THE BEATING HEART

The Heart can beat with

LOVE
DESIRE
PITY
SYMPATHY
FEAR
JEALOUSY
INDIGNATION

THE BEATING HEART

VICTORIA CROSS

WILDSIDE PRESS

THE KISS IN THE WILDERNESS

They were coming up in a closed carriage from Jerico, a jolly, merry, roystering crowd. Melisande whose real name was Eliza, late of the Gaiety theatre, now married to a millionaire, Lord and Lady Hillingford on their honeymoon, an old bachelor Major keen on reckless adventure, and Miss Smith.

To pass the time they were singing comic songs with resounding chorus, which floated out of the open windows and echoed strangely from the stony hills of the wide stretching barren wilderness that lies between Jerico and Jerusalem.

It was a brilliant night with a huge silver moon at the full hanging in the sky above sending its floods of light down upon the lonely waste, in which there was no tree nor flower nor bird: yet something moved at intervals, a curious low four-footed shape with sloping spine and coat so cunningly contrived in spots and lines of brown and white that it matched exactly the patchy, stony hills and clefts and crannies amongst the rocks through which the creatures flitted with their elusive movements.

The exhilarated crowd within the carriage took no notice except one, Miss Smith who was always an exception to whatever the rest might do or be.

The supper at the Jerico Inn before their start had been good with copious libations of the rich Greek wine and now Melisande's golden head was leaning on Hillingford's shoulder while she shrilled out the chorus from her coral mouth and the millionaire's arm was round Lady Hillingford's neck and the Greek wine no doubt was to blame if she was too confused to notice it wasn't her husband's arm. The old Major was frankly overcome and curled up in a quiescent ball in his corner of the great roomy old carriage, only Miss Smith sat quiet and sedate in her grey travelling dress watching the shapes flitting among the rocks in the moonlight. They were hyaenas Miss Smith knew what they were. She was not intoxicated, she was not sleepy. She was not singing comic songs. She sat up straight, alert and watchful.

Her companions did not heed her. They generally left her alone recognizing that while with them she was not of them. At the same time they did not object to her. No one ever objected to Miss Smith. They teased her goodnaturedly because she never drank, smoked, flirted nor swore as they did and used to read and study dingy brown books in the queer languages of the country and she as goodnaturedly smiled and continued to pursue her own quiet way. Among other women she was generally passed over and ignored and considered unattractive because she was generally termed "good" and in these days to be a good woman, is not attractive. A beautiful woman, a fast woman, a fascinating woman, a wicked woman, any adjective almost, sounds interesting but good no. So once having dubbed her good everyone let her alone and she was allowed to wear her crown of Virtue unchallenged and undisturbed.

In person she was rather tall and slender and affected quiet well-fitting tailor made clothes. Her hair was of a warm brown shade and very thick but so quietly done, pressed close to her small head that no one looked twice at it while the frizzed out golden curls, now getting thin from over much dying that flared in a halo round Melisande's head drew every eye. Miss Smith's skin was cool and pale, her eye grave and grey a different thing altogether from the sunny saucy laughing blue beloved by man. Yet the eye had beauty in its calm repose like a clear deep pool in a shady wood. She was 36 though she looked only about 26 and her present and future had been kindly settled for her as old maid by her friends. When she had first joined the touring party, both the married men had attempted to flirt with her after the way of married men but Miss Smith did not care for flirtations with married men and did not want the attentions of the old bachelor Major Mitchell who gallantly offered them. What she did want was locked up in her own soul.

She had been proposed to at 16 and had accepted. He was a young man her father's secretary. The engagement had pursued a tranquil and as Miss Smith privately thought a disappointing course until one evening when as he was leaving her after much long and as she thought boring conversation, she ventured to whisper softly as he took her hand in farewell "Kiss me."

Instantly she was enfolded in his arms and a kiss pressed upon her lips, not an irreverent one but one full of force and electric fire and pressed down so hard that her lips were painfully crushed upon her teeth, under it. When he let her go suddenly she was absolutely white dazed and breathless and involuntarily sank down on the chair nearest her.

The young man's face was white too as they stared for a moment at each other in silence. Not a word was spoken. He retreated silently, swiftly to the door and vanished through it. She sat still where she was until the beating of her heart grew calmer and allowed her to get up. Then as the sense of physical shock passed she smiled. That had been delightful! That was Life! That was Love! That moment compensated her for the preceding boring weeks of her engagement. In that moment she had had her first insight into that stupendous joy that we share with the animals and primitive man alike. Perverted, degraded, chained and beaten down out of sight, as the sexual instinct is by civilization, there are still moments like these of innocent youthful joy in which we see the face of Nature for an instant and realise her tremendous power.

Little Christine Smith went to bed that night profoundly happy. Engagements were not stupid after all. Life was not all dullness. Poets and novelists were right. There was something in existence which was marvelous and golden and glowing and it was love. She adored her fiance now. Had he not in that electric wonderful kiss shown her the majestic Force that he represented? It was overaweing, inspiring. All night she dreamt innocently happily of the kiss that had lifted her to heaven. In the morning there was a letter from him.

Trembling and flushing she had carried it to her room to read alone. His prayer no doubt to her to hasten their marriage so that there might be more and more and more of those heavenly moments. But the letter was not that. *It was an apology.* A craving of pardon for that kiss. A promise that if forgiven he would never, never ever again. Christine could not understand. Grown cold and white she read that astounding letter over and over again and the more she read it the less she understood it. What did he mean? What was wrong? Why was the kiss wrong? It was not, her common sense told her that. It had been just the revelation of his love for her in all its splendid strength and ardour and she loved him for it, and now here was this stupid letter in which he painted himself as a sort of criminal. She was dumbfounded. But one thing was clear. He evidently thought the kiss was very wicked and if she did not agree then he would think her very wicked also. Christine sat very still and cold thinking, the gay mirage that Nature had flung all about her dissipated and gone. Her primitive instincts urged her to go to him and tell him he was mistaken. The kiss was Right and he must take her in his arms and kiss her again and again in exactly the same way give her again that wonderful glimpse of a golden and rose-coloured world of ecstasy. But civilised 16 is rather shy. Christine shrank from facing that cold condemnation that was in the letter, turned upon herself. It seemed so impossible to explain, to find the words to fit all those myriad feelings leaping within herself. She was afraid he would not understand.

At last after hours of thought she folded the letter and put it away. He had said he would come that evening to hear her say she forgave him. She decided she must say nothing but extend to him her pardon as he desired.

For months the engagement went on. Christine secretly hoped that once again his feelings might betray him and that glorious moment come again but it never did.

The engagement was finally broken off and not by him. Christine told him gently that she feared they hardly understood each other well enough for marriage.

The young man mournfully and humbly accepted her decree. To this day he believes that it was that fatal moment (to her so ecstatic) that was his undoing.

There had been several engagements since then on the same dull formal lines and terminated in the same way by her. They had not contained any whirling moments such as the one she had experienced and for the return of which she waited confidently as an astronomer for the return of a comet. This time when it came....

Meanwhile she was not unhappy. She was strong and fleet of foot and clear of eye. She had perfect health in a splendid well knit frame and life was sweet and all the days of this tour through Palestine had been very bright and fair.

She had enjoyed especially this just finished visit to Jerico, going down from Jerusalem in the early summer when the heat was so deadly that not a soul except their own reckless party would venture down there.

The Hotel keeper at Jerusalem had begged them not to go! The season for it was over the heat far too great but they had laughed at him. They had been so cooked they declared a temperature of 110° could not frighten them and the idea of going down down to the scorching plain of Jerico, to the borders of the Dead Sea beneath which lay the sinful Cities of the Plain had a delightful fascination in it.

The road the landlord urged was extremely dangerous. It lay through the wilderness and at this time the Bedouin Arabs were travelling up and down. Caravans and long lines of them fully armed might be met at any point. If go they must an escort of two armed soldiers would be provided for them by the Government. What would be the good of two soldiers against a band of robbers? Hillingford had asked and the landlord had explained "If you have Turkish soldiers with you, no matter how few, it shows you are under the protection of the Sultan of Turkey the head of their religion the Sheik-Islam: they will not lift a hand against their own chief. No one will touch you."

The party consented to take the escort but at the last moment it did not arrive and they would not wait. Finally to the sound of lamentations from their host, they drove away, in the capacious vehicle with a good pair of horses and a single un-armed man as driver. They went by night to avoid the blinding heat of the sun and here they were returning by night by moonlight and the moonlight that falls on the plain of Jerico and on the stony wilderness around it is as hot as English sunlight. The party were well pleased with their visit they had enjoyed it especially Miss Smith. She had liked the journey down down into the simmering bowl of heat, at the bottom of which lay the rich verdant tree filled plain of Jerico and the sparkling blue Salt Lake called the Dead Sea.

The Jerico Inn kept by a Greek where they stayed was a low white building of immensely thick walls and almost hidden from view under the shade of a gigantic fig tree whose wide spreading massive thick leaved boughs filled the court yard with deep delicious shadow green and cool. Here, on their arrival after midnight they had sat and supped at a table neatly spread with bread and cheese and fruit and great jars of honey and the rich heady wines of Greece and while the others had ri-oted and jested and laughed and kissed Miss Smith had sat gazing up through the fig leaves to where between them here and there a great planet burned fiercely in the sky uneclipsed even by the silver light of the moon. She was enjoying it all in her deep calm soul. The next morning the rioters slept late in the cool stone cham-bers of the inn, but she was up while the larks were singing overhead and the whole fair plain of Jerico was smiling in fresh dew and early light. Alone and unafraid and unmolested she found her way down to the edge of the sparkling sea, undressed and bathed in its wonderful blue and limpid waters that would not let her sing and clung round her snowy throat and limbs like the heaviest thickest oil.

Miss Smith thought of all these things now in pleasant retrospect as the carriage lumbered along slowly up the stony road between the hills.

Suddenly a sharp sound the crack of a rifle came stinging through the silence, followed by a terrible thud in front of the carriage. Their driver, doubled up in a sort of ball, fell from his seat and then rolled heavily to the ground, the reins still in his hands. The horses plunged and shied a little as his body fell close by their heels, but they were too hot and weary in that long upward climb to run away. They were star-tled frightened, something had happened but fatigue was greater than any other feeling. They stopped dead still with heaving sweating sides.

The instant the carriage stopped, the occupants who had by now sung them-selves into a state of lethargy, woke up with a shock and the men began to get out. Miss Smith had descended on her side and was first at the side of the fallen driver.

Miss Smith knew all about first aid and she saw here there was no aid to be given. The man was dead. The old Major came to her side. He also knew death when he saw it. "God bless me!" he ejaculated. "This is dreadful, poor fellow! Poor fellow! What's it all mean, eh?"

Miss Smith did not answer, she was looking through the silver space to a long broken line of rocks some 200 yards away. From these, men were running up to them. In a few moments it seemed the carriage in which the two women still sat, huddled together, was surrounded by a circle of Bedouin Arabs. Each one carried a rifle in one hand and a short knife was thrust into the broad sash folded many times round their waist.

Thought is very quick and Miss Smith had time to think even in that alarming moment how handsome and picturesque a crowd they were. Their dark faces were finely carved and featured with brilliant flashing eyes and teeth. On their heads they wore what looked like two enormous rolls of coloured cord, deep red and blue, forming a sort of turban and falling in a twist on their shoulders at the back. A vest of coloured silk and purple Zouave jacket, wide sash and cartridge belt, and loose crimson trousers to somewhat below the knee made up a costume worn with extraordinary grace on beautiful and stately figures of about average height. These men were not specially tall but extremely lithe and well proportioned. They closed round the little English group as leopards encircle antelope. Two of them between them carried the soft limp body of a shot hyaena. They laid it down by the body of the driver. Miss Smith stooped for a moment and stroked softly the exquisite white fur on its chest. Then she straightened herself and looked round on the circle of eager dark faces and asked them in Arabic what they wanted.

And then the whole English party realised that they were helpless and useless in this emergency except for this slim quiet serene person, whom they had laughed at and ignored. She was now the mistress of the situation. Their lives and safety lay in her hands. They could only stand by gaping helplessly while she, thanks to her dingy brown books, parleyed with their enemies.

It looked as if they were in an appalling mess and they depended on her now to get them out of it. The women in the carriage put scared white faces out of the window.

"What do they say, the scoundrels?" queried the Major after Christine in her musical voice had exchanged some sentences with the leader. To Major Mitchell the best man living, if he had a dark skin, was always a scoundrel.

"He says they had no intention of killing our driver," she replied, "but a shot ricochetted from a rock that was aimed at a hyaena."

"Oh come that's good!" said Hillingford, "well then can they help us to get on anywhere?"

"You must remember that is what they *say*," she returned calmly and then she resumed conversing with the Arab leader, while the women in the carriage shivered in the heat and the English men cursed themselves inwardly for having come without the Government guard. The millionaire stole close to Christine's side. "Offer them anything, *anything*, a thousand, ten thousand, if we get safely back to Jerusalem," he whispered shakily. Christine turned her clear eyes upon him. "I do not think *money* is what they want," she replied regarding him steadily. What she thought they did want she did not say.

John Briggs, millionaire, stepped back, white under his Eastern sunburn. His money had smoothed out most ruts in his life. Was it going to fail him now? He glanced at the other two men and it was three very pinched looking faces that stared at each other in the moonlight, while the long glistening barrels of the rifles held by the Arabs sides, almost touched them as the circle drew nearer and the dark eager countenances with their glittering eyes and teeth came thrusting themselves close up to their shoulders.

"Ugly business Jack," muttered Hillingford.

"Scoundrels," repeated the Major whose vocabulary was limited, clenching his fists.

"This is just what the landlord said. Fools we were not to take his advice," said Briggs savagely.

Then they were silent. Christine had finished a long talk with the leading Arab and had now turned to them.

"They say they don't want money nor anything we have with us. That they are not robbers and that the shooting of our driver was an accident. As they have killed him however, they can do nothing without their Sheik's orders. He is called Sheik Lasrali and he has a tent pitched some distance from here in the wilderness and we must all go there with them and hear his orders."

"What cheek! The scoundrels," burst out the Major. Christine's even brows contracted a little.

"Do be careful Major and control yourself," she said, "We are in a bad enough position as it is, don't make it worse."

"How are we to get to this Lasrali?" asked Hillingford.

"We must walk," returned Christine and he thought how well she showed up, standing there in the moonlight, wholly undismayed, quite calm and mistress of herself and talking easily and clearly that difficult gutteral tongue which he had given up studying in despair.

"We have no driver," she went on, "and if we had the carriage couldn't go over that rough ground. It would be overturned directly. We have got to go back some distance in that direction." She pointed far back across the stony waste towards the plain of Jerico whence they had come and the travellers groaned involuntarily. To go back! Further away from the city with its law and order and protection, further into this savage desolation where the moonlight showed nothing but rocks and stones where even the rough rocky grass struggled in vain for existence and here and there bleached bones showed whitely on the ground.

"There is no help for it" she said merely and turned to the carriage. The women in it were sitting white faced and silent but like English women faced with grave emergency their courage rose to meet it. There was no complaint, no shrinking back. They opened the door of the carriage and stepped down on to the stony ground without a word.

The vehicle was packed in all its corners with small handbags and cases, extra cloaks and wraps and sunshades. The Arabs peered in curiously jabbering amongst themselves. There was a hasty consultation between the travellers as to whether they could carry anything with them. The Gaiety girl, Melisande, prayed for her handbag. It had all her make up in it. Lady Hillingford could not bear parting from her small flat case. Hillingford hastily opened his bag and extracted his favorite razor. Miss Smith went to hers and pulled out her Arabic dictionary.

"Don't take much," she advised. "It's so hot and we have a long way to walk. The Arabs are going to leave a guard and the carriage and all its contents will be perfectly safe. I have told them we must take the horses out and take them with us. The Sheik will have water and food and rest when we get there."

While the women fussed over their luggage, anxious as human beings always are about trifles even with the great issues of life and death hanging over them, and the Arabs sat down a little way off watching them with an amused smile curling their dark lips and their rifles held across their knees, the three men and Christine stood for a moment together at the horses' heads.

"I wonder whether we're wise," Hillingford asked, "in giving in like this? Suppose we said we would not go?"

"The alternative is for us all to sit here under a guard while two of the Arabs go off with a message to the Sheik and ask for orders." Christine answered, she had evidently discussed this with the chief already, "but you see he might be ages coming back. Perhaps he wouldn't come till the morning and we'd get awfully tired waiting here and the horses would get no water. Then he says the Sheik would be sure to send for us, so we'd have to go in the end."

"Why should he send for us, damn him?" This from the Major.

"The leader says he would not mind the men going on but he would be sure to want to see the three ladies!"

"Scoundrel!" shouted the Major.

"I think we had better go and make no trouble about it," said Christine, "we may be able to reason things out with Lasrali."

The men nodded. There seemed no way out. An Arab came up and took out the two horses, weary and dejected with the long toil. Christine patted their necks and the Arab led them off the roadway. Next came another Arab strung about with various small articles belonging to the English that he had been deputed to carry by the leader. Hillingford and his wife followed, then Briggs and Melisande, then the Major and Christine and this small column of English was flanked on each side by a guard of six Arabs.

Christine turned and glanced back as they were starting. Two motionless Arabs sat on the box seat of the carriage, their rifles on their knees. Side by side on the ground lay the dead driver and the dead hyaena mingling their blood in a small dark pool on the road.

Out into the wilderness. Away from even the road, that wild desolate and inhospitable as it is, has at least, each end in civilization. But in the wilderness itself that stretches between the proud city of Jerusalem and the fair plain of Jerico there one can see the face of Loneliness itself and feel Starvation and Death lurking among those never ending ridges of whitish rock rising from the arid, waterless plain. The African desert with its soft films of sand, its glorious mirage seems homelike by contrast with it. The American desert with unbroken miles of sagebrush and its alkali pools seems inviting ground in comparison. In the wilderness there is nothing but solitude and stone and hyaenas grown fat on the corpses of wayfarers.

Doggedly and in silence the little party went on. The two wives in their thin high heeled shoes and silk stockings suffered most. The men and Christine walked easily on flat heels over the loose stones and uneven surface. But no one of them made any sound of discontent. Melisande and Eva Hillingford stumbled along awkwardly and painfully but bravely and the curls on their forehead and the silk blouses on their chests were soaked through with sweat in the hot still air.

Apprehension as to their possible fate had got its teeth well into them now. Leaving the road, their only friend and guide, had brought them to a sense of their utter helplessness. Even if left now unmolested, they could not find their way back to it, they could only wander about amongst these everlasting gleaming rocks, each one exactly like another till they died.

After a little while physical fatigue and pain shut out much reflection on other things. They were intolerably thirsty and their limbs ached from that curious rough walking similar to going up hill on an English beach. The Arabs were not inconsiderate and did not even hurry them. Only once when the Major lagged behind one of the guard pressing on their heels poked the nuzzle of a rifle against his shoulder blades. After that, rather than have it happen again, he stepped out more briskly.

The first light of the dawn showed faintly in the East, when the Arab leader pointed out to the white weary crowd toiling on some large dark objects not very far away.

"Lasrali's tents," he said.

It seemed as they came nearer quite a large encampment altogether a great number of tents pitched near to a ridge of rock which slightly overhanging made a sort of rough shed. Against this were grouped various animals, camels, horses, donkeys and goats, some lying down others standing round a heap of fodder put down for them. Christine went forward and spoke earnestly with the Arab leading the horses: making him promise to allow them to lie down and to give them plenty of food and water as they could take it. He laughed showing all his glittering teeth in the bright moonlight.

"Lasrali would be very angry with me if I did not look after them. He loves horses." What a relief those words carried to her mind. A man who loved horses could not be wholly bad. She fell back and told the good news to the others. They were just on the outside of the encampment now. Most of its occupants had retired apparently, but a long line of cooking fires burnt redly still upon the ground. The chief man who had so far all along spoken with Christine, gave his charges over to the guard and disappeared into the largest of the tents to know his master's wishes. It was only a few minutes before he returned and ushered them all in, holding back the tent flaps for them and then bringing up the rear himself.

It was a large and roomy tent well carpeted and with masses of silken cushions lying about. Also there were little tables at which if sitting on a cushion on the floor, one could comfortably write and read.

Lasrali himself was seated in one of those capacious black wood chairs inlaid with mother of pearl, so familiar in Damascus. Wearing a snow white burnous, edged with gold embroidery and a gold band encircling the hood of it, just above his black brows he presented a kingly and dignified appearance. His face was handsome in the typical Arab way. Olive skinned and oval with refined aristocratic features and large dark eyes. In age he appeared about 38. In one rather white and slender hand he held a long stemmed pipe which he appeared to have been peacefully smoking when disturbed.

12

As soon as the worn weary captives were ushered in, he rose from his seat, bowed slightly and then immediately resumed it, ordering one of his Arabs to bring forward cushions for his visitors. When these were brought the three women sank down gratefully upon them, the men taking their stand behind them until Lasrali waved them with a more decided gesture to be seated also. Then he called up the leader to stand beside him, and set himself to listen attentively to the man's story, pulling occasionally at his pipe and asking now and then a quiet question.

The Arab leader went on with his interminable relation for endless time as it seemed to the wearied English. With the exception of Miss Smith, they could none of them understand a word and they were so dazed and sleepy with heat and fatigue that the conversation came to their ears only in an unmeaning blur. Christine was tired too, but her head was clear and she sat bright eyed and upright on her cushion listening intently to every word that was uttered. Much of the conversation's meaning she missed of course. It is impossible for a stranger however well he knows a language to catch all that passes between two others, not addressing him but talking rapidly to each other, but the drift of it she gathered very well. At one time when the leader said something as to money she took her courage in both hands and ventured to re-inforce his statement.

"There is a gentleman here," she said, indicating Briggs, "who will pay anything you like to ask in money for our release."

Lasrali regarded her in silence but did not reply and the leader turned on her saying:

"My master is very rich man, he does not seek money. He might be pleased however to take a white wife."

"The dream of my life has been to win a white woman who is also a lady," supplemented Lasrali in a very low tone, "no sum of money can weigh against such a dream."

Christine did not translate any of these sentences into English. They sank into her heart and set it beating. In defiance of something within her that seemed holding her back, she seized hold of the old phrases and stated them as one who speaks from a sense of duty.

"The English are a mighty people. We are few but if any of us are injured, a great army will come to avenge us."

She thought she saw the faint flicker of a smile pass over Lasrali's face that he was too courteous to wholly indulge in. The leader was not so ceremonious however. He laughed openly.

"Your country used to be great and protect its subjects. It is too lazy to do that now. Besides my master cannot be found in his native mountains and the captive men would be killed and scattered to the winds of heaven long before help came and the captive women would be—"

The expression made the blood fly flaming all over Christine's face and Lasrali sharply reprimanded the Arab leader.

"Do not talk to the lady at all," he said with anger. "Confine your conversation to me," and he motioned him to come closer to his chair.

After a long discussion between them Lasrali at last waved him to one side and addressing Christine direct asked her and the other two ladies to get up and approach him. This they did, Christine springing up at once and the other two wearily dragging themselves to their feet. Then they stood in a line before him and the Arab regarded them all with grave attentive eyes. Dusty and tired, with rumpled hair and damp faces, in their rather bright coloured clothes, hatless and with arms and necks bare in the intense heat, neither Lady Hillingford who was 25 and pale and dark, nor Melisande who had no age and was of the flamboyant type, looked their best and being conscious of this did not improve matters by their expressions. Melisande trying to get up her footlight smile and Lady Hillingford frankly weary and disdainful. It was on Christine that the Arab's quiet gaze rested longest. Trim, elegant, apparently untired, her clear pale skin rendered still paler by the heat, her large eyes burning with keen interest and power, her lips, glowing red, her thick hair unruffled in its soft close waves about her head, she certainly presented the most pleasing aspect of the three. Her gaze was fixed unwaveringly upon the handsome face turned to her. She looked exactly what she felt, intensely interested. After a lengthened survey which was in no way rude nor impudent, only evidently extremely critical and observant of the minutest details, he turned to his attendant and told him to conduct all the English to a private tent and look after them except the lady who spoke Arabic and she should follow them directly. Christine looked at her companions with her cheerful smile and translated this adding, "Go ahead and leave me. I'll come as soon as I can."

They did not like seeming to desert her, but she had become so much their leader and director in the last few hours and she seemed so perfectly unafraid of the whole situation that they solemnly filed out after the Arab in silence.

The tent was now empty except for the handsome seated form and herself standing before him, a slender, graceful English figure in her simple grey clothes. The light from the great swinging center lamp fell on her thick brown hair and showed a soft wavering colour in her cheeks as she gazed steadily at her captor. She felt no fear as she heard the others withdraw. She did not know what was going to happen to her, no word in the long conversation had indicated what her fate might be and she knew herself absolutely defenceless but her whole mind had been seized as it were by a great expectancy and there was no room for any other feeling. Physically she was in those moments intensely alive: every sense seemed at its highest power. Her eyes took in every detail of the face and form opposite her, her ears were conscious of the faintest rustle and click of the curtain behind her as they fell to shutting her in, her nostrils quivered to the strange scent of tobacco and camel, coffee and wood fire, in the tent. Her whole being seemed rising on tip-toe to go forward to something she did not know. Lasrali rose from his seat and approached her. She did not retreat. Then in a single sweep of his arm he had drawn her close up to his breast, he bent his head and pressed his lips down hard on hers.

Then suddenly she knew that here now, whirling down upon her through the space of twenty years, was again the wonderful moment she had known at 16 and never refound. It was here now. It was hers again. Her head was pressed back on his arm. She could not move. Again the pain on her mouth. Again the realization of being in the presence of a tremendous Force and that not a destructive but an august beneficent force, the constructive force of Life itself. Again that glimpse before her eyes of something wonderful, something majestic and utterly beyond the petty details of everyday existence. For the moment she seemed united to something vast, eternal, primaeval, as indeed she was, to the Impulse of Life itself that causes the whole universe to roll on through its countless aeons. Her eyes gazed up to the dark beauty of those above her but she did not see them with their lids half closed over them and the straight black brows contracted into one line almost as with severe physical pain above them. She saw before her mental vision the magnificence of triumphal Life sweeping up towards her to engulf her in its stupendous onrush.

It was only for an instant: She was released suddenly and staggered slightly, clutching at the central tent pole for support and white and trembling just as she had been on that other evening long ago. But her eyes were shining still with the joy of the vision and she smiled at Lasrali now gravely regarding her. He took her arm and led her up to his own vacant chair into which he gently pressed her. Then bending over her he began to speak slowly and distinctly so that she caught every word.

"Listen. I want you. For the others I do not care. As you know I am an Arab and not like the English supposed to have only one wife. I can have a number but as it happens I have none now. If you will stay and be my wife, I will let all your companions go. I will give them a driver and a guard and they will go safely on their way to Jerusalem. Nothing of theirs will be taken and I will send two of my Arabs to explain the shooting."

He stopped, waiting for her reply and Christine in the crisis of her fate seemed suddenly struck dumb. The immensity of her feelings, the intense desire to express all that was surging up in her soul seemed to paralyse her utterance as a volume of water gets choked by its own pressure in the narrow neck of a vessel from which it is struggling to escape. She, the glib interpreter for others, she, the student who had read Arab poetry by the hour was now tongue tied and silent, unable to utter one little word of love or encouragement to the man bending over her. She thought the beauty of his face so perfect, its expression now so infinitely soft and tender, that she longed to throw her arms about his neck and tell him that she loved him and would those words have been any less true, any more exaggerated an expression than when an English society girl says, "I love you," to a man she is going to marry, after a three weeks' engagement?

Rather, the truth of it was so intense in Christine's case and the realisation of it so overawing that her lips were locked and her limbs seemed inert. She struggled as we struggle in dreams to speak but not a single world would come to her aid. She could only look and look back to the eyes above her. Her dilated, appealing gaze might have been one of helpless, fascinated terror and her heart thumping so violently in her bosom blanched her face and lips.

A shade of disappointment came over Lasrali's countenance.

"You will stay to save your friends?" he repeated and Christine managed to force her trembling lips to a weak, yes.

"Aiwa."

Lasrali gave a deep sigh as of relief and straightened himself. His face relapsed into its habitual gravity as he said:

"I see you are very frightened but there is no need. In my tent you will not be hurt or grieved. You will be safe, protected, I believe happy. I shall try with all my force to make you so. You are very tired now, go and rest; eat and sleep. Peace be with you."

Again Christine tried to respond but the whole view of this love and life so suddenly forced upon her seemed too great for her to assimilate and to find quickly the suitable words a vehicle for her thoughts. And the moment for her to speak and accept seemed maliciously to have gone before she could grasp it.

If it was impossible for her to speak while he bent over her, his face suffused with tenderness, it seemed still more hopeless to do so now when he had drawn a little away and his usual calm and dignity had enfolded him.

She hesitated clasping her hands, not as he fancied in supplication to him, but to those unseen powers that were holding her, preventing her disclosing her feeling towards him. Her mind was staggered and as we fail when suddenly we come into view of a colossal mountain or a huge giant tree, to summon words in which to describe our admiration, because words seem so inadequate, so did Christine fail now.

Lasrali did not touch her again but with a grave gesture, waved her to the door of the tent, the curtains of which he himself held back that she might pass through.

With a look of intense gratitude, admiration and love, which he translated as one of final appeal, she passed out and he was left alone.

*   *   *   *   *

When Christine entered the other tent, the rest of the party were seated in the centre, round a piece of carpet on which stood a coffee pot of steaming coffee, a jug of goat's milk, white bread as good as in the Jerico hotel and a pile of dates.

They raised jaded looking enquiring faces to her as she joined the circle and sat down.

"It's all right. You are quite safe. Give me some coffee and I'll tell you."

"Hurrah!" exclaimed Briggs. "Well you are splendid. What does he say?"

"He says, first we must all sleep here and rest until it's cool to-morrow afternoon. He will then send you all with a good driver and an armed escort up to Jerusalem and an Arab who will explain all about the shooting and see that the proper people are sent after our driver's body, which will be guarded till they come." She paused and drank up her coffee. A relieved sigh rose from the others, from all except the Major who would not look relieved. He glared fiercely into his coffee cup in silence.

"How wonderful!" said Lady Hillingford.

"Good fellow," from her husband.

"Thank God," said the millionaire.

"Well, he's a darling," declared Melisande.

Then Christine quietly threw her bombshell.

"Yes, only he says one of the women must stay."

"Scoundrel," shouted the Major, banging his cup down on the carpet.

"Ah, I *thought* so," murmured Lady Hillingford turning very white.

The two husbands looked at each other across the coffee without a word.

"Which one does he want?" asked Melisande drawing out her little mirror from the bag on her lap and puffing out her golden locks at the side of her head with her jewelled fingers.

"Me," replied Christine.

"*You?*" exclaimed both ladies at once with an emphasis which was not at all complimentary.

"Yes: seems strange, doesn't it?" returned Christine tranquilly, sinking her white even teeth into her dates with keen satisfaction. She was evidently going to enjoy her supper to the full.

All eyes turned on her. Her companions stared at her in those moments as if they had never seen her before. And indeed it was a new Christine from the one they had been travelling with. The primaeval woman was rising in her in all her strength and glory and arming her with new and wonderful weapons. In her skin which had a curious transparency was kindled a lovely rose flush, her eyes were no longer still dark pools but rather wells of moving fire, her lips were redder than Melisande's painted ones. As she sat her slender body rose full of proud grace from her cushion seat.

There was a long pause, full of tension. Somehow the ladies looked displeased and the men not less concerned than before. Melisande was the first to break the silence.

"What did you say?" she asked abruptly as Christine continued to eat calmly and cheerfully.

"Said I'd stay."

"Said you would stay?" gasped the men together.

"Yes, of course. I wasn't going to get you all shot and Eva and Sandy kept as prisoners as well as myself. I didn't see the use."

"Oh, but look here, we can't stand this," broke out Hillingford. "Do you think we could go back and save ourselves at your expense like that?"

"Well, what would you propose?" asked Christine pouring more milk into her coffee.

"Er—well, I—er—don't know—I should think they'd never dare to—to—" he stopped.

"I don't know either but they might dare a good lot. I heard a great many cheering references to 'Dead men tell no tales,' while the leader was talking to him. He seemed to think it was a splendid plan for you three men to be shot and then for Lasrali to disappear into the wilderness with us three women after duly rewarding his faithful followers with our horses, carriage, bags, and jewelry and burying the driver under a rock. It sounded a most engaging programme and I was afraid each minute Lasrali would accept it. But he wouldn't."

"Did you offer him all he liked to ask if he would let us *all* go?" asked Briggs.

"I did and he said it had been the dream of his life to—to marry a white woman and a lady and he would not give it up for any amount of money."

"Scoundrel," exclaimed the Major.

"Did you say that although we seemed a small party we had all the power of England and the law behind us and he would certainly suffer very much if he injured us?"

"I did: and he said England wasn't much good now and didn't protect her people worth a cent. Besides which nobody could possibly get at him in the wilderness until—until, well, until he'd realised his dream."

"Devil! Devil!" shouted the Major who had at last got on to another word.

The others all sat pale and silent. The tremendous end of their journey to the Dead Sea taken so thoughtlessly and gaily was coming close up to them now and appalled them.

It was Hillingford who spoke first.

"I don't know what you others think about it but personally I feel I'd rather stay here and be shot than save myself at a woman's expense. Damn it, I say, we *can't* go back and leave you here."

"Our wives, Hillingford, our wives, we've got to think of them," murmured Briggs. He doubtless did think of his wife, but also somewhere at the back of his mind he had the feeling that Eternal Justice would be better satisfied by Miss Smith becoming an Arab's bride than by John Briggs with all his millions being murdered in the wilderness.

"If I know Eva," Hillingford returned hotly, "she'd die here with me rather than sneak out of a thing like this."

Lady Hillingford looked back at her husband. Her face was dead white but she knew what she had to do and say and played up to her caste.

"Certainly, Will, I'll stay. I have no doubt you can finish me with a rock or a knife."

Christine looked over to him with a smile in her now lovely eyes. Then having finished an excellent meal, she sat back on her cushion and wiped her pink tipped fingers on her little handkerchief. Then she stretched out a small hand to Hillingford.

"It's most awfully good of you Lord Hillingford and I do appreciate it. But I should simply hate for all our lives to be wasted. I should want to do the same and stay and save you, in any case but as it is you needn't worry at all. You can all go off with clear consciences. We came out for adventures and this is the biggest we've had. It's mine principally and I'm going to take it. I think Lasrali hasn't been half bad in spite of what the Major says. He has very self sacrificingly picked out the plainest and least attractive woman simply because she's free and the others have husbands. I like him and I'm going to stay and marry him."

This was another bombshell amongst them that left them gasping. Only Melisande did not seem surprised. She watched Christine with a little malicious smile.

"Good heavens!" was all Hillingford seemed able to answer and the distress on his face hardly lightened. Briggs was candidly and openly pleased. It had been an awful moment for him when he really thought Death was coming for him through his stockade of money-bags.

"Very plucky, I call it," he said, "daring little devil, isn't she Sandy?"

"Oh, very," returned Melisande getting out her cigarette case and lighting up.

Suddenly the Major banged both clenched fists down on the carpet square making the coffee cups dance and jingle.

"You an English woman going to marry that devil and *like it*. Faugh!"

In his indignation he tried to struggle to his feet but being short and fat and seated on a cushion he found this very difficult and nearly rolled over into the coffee cups. Christine sprang to her feet and offered him her hand.

18

"I think we're all dead tired," she said, "let's go to bed and talk in the morning."

The rest of the circle broke up. They were tired beyond all words and got up and approached thankfully the great square at the back of the tent where rugs were unrolled and a quantity of cushions laid out. They ranged themselves in the following order. Lady Hillingford, then her husband, then the millionaire, then his wife, then next her in the outside Miss Smith. The Major would have none of them. He stalked up to the capacious bed and took his cushion and small rug.

"I despise you," he said in a fierce undertone to Miss Smith as he grabbed his pillow.

"Sorry," replied Christine and threw herself full length beside Melisande. She longed for rest and a cessation of talk and discussion, to lie still in the darkness and listen to the Voice of Nature in her ear and feel the kiss of Life burning on her lips.

They drew the great rug which they shared in common over them, for with the dawn a little chill was coming into the air.

"Put out the light as you pass, Major," called Briggs, and the Major did so throwing his rug and cushion down as far from the others as he could get. No one spoke any more and sleep came down heavily like a great cloud upon them and enfolded them. Except (as usual) Christine. Stretched out still and looking into the soft darkness, she lay and thought.

Here after all these years, winging its way to her across the gulf of time and space had come again the joy she had known when on the threshold of life.

She had come into the barren desert which gives nothing neither shade nor rest nor water nor food, and it had given her this.

How strangely things happened; she had joined this touring party, hoping for fun and adventure, all the amusing little adventures of travel and suddenly she had stumbled into the biggest adventure that could happen to her that would change her whole life.

She was, what so very few of us are, free from the necessity of consideration for others. She was without relations, home or family ties. Without any dear ones to regret or that would regret her. In the twenty years that had intervened between that first engagement and the present time, one by one every one that belonged to her or who loved her had been taken from her. She had felt the extreme loneliness of this grow upon her and had wildly resented it at times, but here now she saw that it was enviable. Without remorse or regret, she was free to accept this great experience, now she had come face to face with it. She had nothing to hold her nor restrain her from going forward to it. There was nothing in the life behind her to hold out a single detaining hand. She had not even a pet nor a house that needed attention and arrangement.

She was one of those single women with a sufficient income to dress well and live in the best hotels who spent her time studying, motoring, dancing, amusing herself in all legitimate, civilized ways, travelling widely and looking, always looking for something. With some of them if they are plain and stupid it is love they are looking for, sometimes only a kiss. Christine had never had to seek for love and kisses she could have had by dozens. It was because she was looking for a particular kind of love, a special sort of kiss, that the search had been long. She did not seek brutality nor cruelty, those are totally different from though often confused with force, intensity. The real true strength of Love that is striving to create Life in a beloved object that is what she had been seeking and had now found and she could not see that she had to make any particular sacrifice for it. She admired the grave dignity and beauty of the man himself and she had felt that strange sharp call of his individuality to hers, which is after all the basis of all love between the sexes whether civilized or uncivilized. The one quality which to her was one absolute essential in any man she was to love, tenderness and kindness to animals seemed assured by what his servant had said. Had she really known anything more of her father's secretary, than she knew now of Lasrali? She could have married him for the sake of that golden moment in his arms and she was now going to marry Lasrali for exactly the same reason. In her eyes it was quite as good a reason as marrying to obtain a house in town, a settled income or a title. She saw very clearly that Nature, cruel as she is in the deaths, disease, pain and all the woes she sends upon us and the animals has yet in her hands for all created things this one supreme joy and consolation for all the suffering of life, the joy of simple, natural unrestrained love. No animals fail to realise this and few men and women in a natural state, but in a civilized state there are hundreds of thousands who live, marry, suffer and die without one glimpse of this Eternal Truth.

So far Christine had steadily avoided marrying anyone, between whom and herself there did not seem to be that strange wild magnetism, that irresistible call and challenge to the senses, getting out of her numerous engagements as best she could and submitting to being angrily and furiously called a jilt, which she knew was not true. She was simply one looking for gold and consistently refusing the dross that was pressed upon her in its place.

Lasrali did not sleep that night. All through the remaining hours he sat wide eyed in his chair, sometimes drawing at his pipe but more often idle staring down at the carpet that kept the stony dust of the wilderness from his fine narrow high arched feet. A very hardy struggle was going on within him and he was fighting bravely against the greatest power in the Universe, outside that still greater power that has been given to the soul of man.

Several times his wearied attendant outside raised the tent flap a tiny bit and looked in only to see his master still sitting there as a statue, lost in thought.

It is absurd to limit the good and bad impulses in man by any creed, caste, or colour. The human soul has no such limits. Nobleness, generosity, self-sacrifice, dwell indiscriminately in black, yellow, red, and white races alike. Evil, also is scattered impartially through the whole of humanity as witness the loathsome cruelties and barbarities committed by men of our own time and race under the name of Scientific Research which surpass in horror anything done by savage tribes.

At last when the morning was fairly on its way, he summoned his Arab.

"Are the English still sleeping?"

"Yes, they all sleep very soundly: a good time to kill the men now if you wish."

Lasrali lifted his hand in protest, his brows contracting.

"Listen. When the English wake, take them water for washing and all they need. Then a good meal. While they eat, come and rouse me if I should be sleeping. When they finish their meal, bring them here to me."

20

The Arab bowed and went away muttering. Lasrali, exhausted, passed through the curtains to his inner tent to sleep.

Although Christine had slept less than the others she was the first to awake, when the light was sinking in the tent and the flush of sunset was stealing over the wilderness, softening all its grim, glaring whiteness. She looked round with a feeling of surprise that the day had vanished, they had slept it away. It seemed strange to be waking to the rose of sunset instead of the rose of dawn as she was accustomed to do. She lifted herself from the rugs and looked at the sleepers beside her. Hillingford was the only one whose eyes were open and as he met her glance he smiled and as if by common consent they both rose, very quietly so as not to disturb the others and went out of the tent together, passing by the Major still soundly asleep by the door.

The encampment outside was an animated scene, cooking fires were sparkling everywhere and Arabs coming and going between them preparing the evening meal. The line of camels and other animals were feeding leisurely under their rock shelter, all the tent doors were open except the great double one, really two tents, joined together, one behind the other, which belonged to Lasrali. Of these the door flaps were closed and fastened and two Arabs sat on the ground before them.

Christine looked out on it all curiously and smelt the scent of the wood fires rising in the hot still air with a curious leaping of the heart. Why is it that the scent of the camp fire affects all or nearly all mankind with a strange feeling like nostalgia? Is it because on its fragrance our senses are borne back to primaeval times when our first camp fires smoked in the untamed forest?

She glanced across to Lasrali's tent and the sight of its closed door struck her with a sense of loneliness. Her life henceforth would lean upon him. This scene that she looked upon would be its outside shell but there was nothing in it that she cared about except himself.

She turned to Hillingford who stood beside her. The Arabs about them glanced at them sideways, but the Mahomedan from his earliest years is taught not to stare and the long dark eyes were drooped again immediately over boiling kettle, or rice bowl as if they had seen nothing unusual.

"There are just one or two things I should like you to do for me," she said gently, "if you will."

"Of course, I will, anything," he returned gazing at her in the soft rose light that fell all about them from the tinted sky. How wonderfully well she was looking he thought with no toilet made nor adjuncts of any kind. He did not realise how the great force of expectant life was awakened and moving within her, painting her cheeks and lips, kindling and softening her eyes.

"You know I have no near relations," she went on, "so there's no one to see or to tell about me, but I should like the money I have to be safeguarded. Will you be my trustee and look after it for me? And re-invest the income, so that in the future, if there should be any—any, well if it's wanted it will be there. In my bag when you go back to the carriage you will find a small packet of all my papers, bank book, check book, etc. Will you take possession of it. That will give you all the details. And send me back by one of the Arabs my little case of clothes. I shall want that here."

"I'll do anything and everything," he returned, "but you must authorize me about the money here," and he drew out his pocket book and gave it to her. "Write down there that you wished me to act for you. Here's a pen." He gave her his own stylographic and she looked at it for a moment in silence.

"Isn't this all funny? Doing this civilized sort of business out here in this wilderness. What an end we have had to our tour!"

"Yes, it's awful," groaned Hillingford, "I shall never forgive myself or feel the same again." Christine had seated herself on a great stone and was writing rapidly in the pocket book all that she thought was necessary. When it was done, she handed up the book and pen to him.

"Will that do?"

Hillingford read it through.

"That's all right," he said and shut the book and replaced it. "But we shall send after you and rescue you as soon as we get back."

Christine still seated put her hand round her knees and stared over the small space that intervened to the closed tent door of Lasrali.

"Do you remember your Roman History?" she said slowly after a minute. "You remember how the Romans carried off the Sabine women and how after a time the Sabine husbands and fathers came after them to rescue them and the Sabine women came out and said they were happy with their Roman husbands and didn't want to be rescued? It was too late. Well it's the same now. I am sure it will be too late. Besides this I am a sort of hostage. If you come after me to rescue me I believe you won't find me because Lasrali will go far, far away in the mountains and hide."

"But surely he could be found. We could get an army to scour the place," remonstrated Hillingford in hot desperation.

Christine shook her head.

"It might be possible to find and punish him but what about me? I should think I should be killed when the news first came to him he was being followed and don't you see he has us all in his power *now*? If he lets you go, you are on parole, as it were. You can't pursue him afterwards," Hillingford groaned, then he burst out, "He's no right to keep you."

"No, but I am staying of my own free will. Don't attempt to rescue me. You will only make fearful trouble if you do and it seems to be dishonourable when he has had you in his power and let you go. Be quite happy about me, really. I have had so many years of ordinary civilized life I am quite prepared to accept this adventure as a change and make the best of it."

Hillingford was silent, staring down at the ground.

"Do you despise me, too, like the Major?" she asked with a little laugh.

"Good heavens, no, I think you are a heroine. Of course, I know whatever you may say, you are only doing it for us!"

Christine's brows contracted.

Again this wall of hopeless misunderstanding. She could not clear it away. She could not explain to him for he would never understand. They spoke the same language, they were of the same country, class and creed, yet she felt further from him, in a way, than she did from the stranger who was their host.

Hillingford who was girt about with conventions and civilization got on very well with the half of Christine that was conventional, civilized woman, the other half the simple, natural primitive woman he would not have been able to understand at all.

Christine did not attempt further explanation all she said was:

"Well, remember the Sabine women and don't rescue me. I don't want it. I think it would be dishonourable and extremely dangerous. When I want civilization again I'll find a way of getting back to it. Now, promise. Then I shall feel safer and happier," and very reluctantly Hillingford promised.

The rosy glow was fading, stars sparkled in it here and there. In the East a great pale moon came up reminding them of the approaching hour of departure.

In silence they walked back to the tent. The door was open and an Arab was lighting the central lamp, while two others were spreading out a meal on the carpet. The women were arranging their hair before scraps of looking-glass and the men sat moody and silent watching the Arabs at work.

It was a short and quiet meal, less lively than their supper last night.

There seemed nothing more to be said. No one seemed to have any ideas, or to wish to speak. A sullen sort of apathy had settled on them all as if they were a flock of overdriven sheep. Christine alone looked radiant and clear-eyed and sat looking through the door of the tent towards that other one of which she could just see the closed flaps. At last she saw movement about it. Arabs went in carrying coffee and Arabs came out and at last one crossed the space to their tent and entered.

"The horses are refreshed and ready. All is now prepared for your departure and our Master would be pleased if you will come to his tent."

Not knowing yet whether they were all going to be executed at the last moment or not the English all rose and followed the Arab out of their tent across the now moonlit space to the other one and were ushered gravely in.

Lasrali was standing to receive them. The audience was to be short so no cushions were prepared nor offered, of which the Major was very glad. They filed in. Christine as the interpreter and the only one who could understand was pushed a little forward and stood in front of the rest. Her eyes alight, her cheeks and lips glowing, her form full of elastic strength, she looked as she felt in the first flush of womanhood. Her face was smiling as she looked up at him and Lasrali looked down at her as a man dying of thirst looks at a crystal spring. Then he began to speak very clearly and restrainedly.

"I am an Arab and a host is a host, and guests are guests. I tell you now you are all free. Last night I made conditions I should not have done. They do not exist this evening. With my escort you will all proceed to Jerusalem and may peace be with you."

He stopped and Christine, paling a little, repeated it in English.

Then Lasrali approached her a step nearer and added: "Sacred is the law of hospitality. I infringed it last night. I touched this lady. To her I apologise."

Utter silence. Christine stood as if actually turned to ice or stone. Her color fled. She gazed up at Lasrali as if he were demented. Her companions to whom the words conveyed nothing grew cold with fear. What now? What in heaven's name had he said? Was all that first palaver some ghastly joke? Had he now suggested they should be eaten alive or what? They gazed at Christine, longing for her to speak and fully prepared for the worst. Her face was a study of astonishment, agony and despair. The Major couldn't stand it. He went up behind her and shook her arm.

"What's he said now? The scoundrel!"

Lasrali bent towards her with grave kindness.

"Perhaps you do not understand. You are free. Go with your friends. I regret that your beauty last night overcame me."

Christine still stood white and silent and trembling. Was it possible? Here again the very idea, the actual words that had ruined her happiness at 16! Here in this man of different race and caste and blood, country and creed, the same misunderstanding. Were men all alike? Was it only Woman who saw clearly back to the primaeval fount of things and recognized in passion the joyous force of life?

"Christine!" it was Lady Hollingford's voice sharp and thin. She was delicate and nervous and she felt she could bear the strain no longer. "Do tell us what he says, whatever it is!"

In a flash Christine saw how this little accident of knowing the language put them all in her power. Her friends, their safety, Lasrali, his reputation, were all her toys.

For the moment the temptation came to her to mistranslate his words. Just to say he dismissed them as had been arranged and was keeping her. The primaeval woman fighting for her ends prompted this. That would satisfy all these civilized fools and they would go and leave her in peace with the heroine's halo round her head. It would be so difficult otherwise perhaps to stay.

But the impulse was pushed aside instantly by her feelings of truth and honour and responsibility to those who trusted her. Also she would not rob Lasrali of the credit for his fine feelings and his self-sacrifice.

Stammering and hesitating because of the amazement gripping her, she gave out his words in English exactly as he had spoken them and the relief of the others was mixed with surprise.

"Well, that's all right! What's the matter with you?" asked Lady Hillingford, but Melisande only laughed.

"Please leave me now I desire rest," Lasrali said.

"Do thank him for us and tell him how grateful we are," Hillingford said and Christine mechanically turned his words into Arabic. Slipping, slipping from her she saw the golden moment, never to be captured again. The English are not a graceful people. They tried to bow and salute Lasrali who stood there reposeful and dignified but they were not very good at it and in a sort of huddled bunch they got through the tent curtains. The Major marched out with flat defiance.

"Showed the white feather after all, didn't dare to touch us, thought so, damned scoundrel!" was his farewell remark.

Christine was the last to leave. The others had preceded her and the curtains had fallen to behind them. Her hand was on the dangling fringes. She looked back. The tent was empty. At the other side of it were the curtains dividing off Lasrali's sleeping tent. Through them he had disappeared. Should she? Dare she? Race after that fleeting, golden moment which was now eluding her for the second time? Behind her lay all those years of an existence she knew so well. Almost every form of civilised amusement that a modern age provides had been hers. And love in all its delicate restrained civilised ways had been offered her again and again but there had seemed something tame and flat about it all. Before her stood Life in another dress or rather in an unashamed barbaric nakedness which had some strength and glory about it. Above all it was something new. She seemed in those seconds to visualise it as a dancing, laughing figure, taunting her, daring her to come after it. And she would dare. Beyond the further curtains was burning a great electric force that was calling to every nerve and pulse and fibre of her frame pulling her irresistibly to itself.

The curtains dropped from her nerveless fingers. Swift, silent as a shadow, she passed across the space and drew back the curtains that had closed behind Lasrali. A dim light burned in the tent. Beyond she saw his unrolled bed. He himself was standing still gazing at the ground. He turned and saw her as she entered, not weak nor white nor trembling nor hesitant now, but alive, determined, triumphant, glowing, expanding, the future mother of a bold and hardy race. Eyes shining, she advanced towards him with outstretched hands.

"Lasrali! don't send me away! I want to stay here with you!"

A flash came over his face as of some great enlightenment. He put both his hands on her shoulders and gazed keenly into her eyes but hers did not waver. They glowed and glowed carrying their message straight to his.

"Is it true?" he asked.

"Yes, I swear it by the Koran."

Over his face so superbly gifted by Nature, swept that wonderful, all enveloping softness and sweetness that filled her with ecstasy.

"Then the dream of my life is realised."

"And mine," said Christine.

25

COLOUR

Circumstances sometimes make us virtuous against our will.

George Morris was pottering about at the back of the dusty, dingy little picture shop, while the dealer had gone to fetch the picture backing George had come in for, when he noticed set away on a shelf a little sketch and paused before it fascinated. It was a most attractive little thing, all red: everything in it was a delightful warm, rich, glowing crimson. The background was red—the interior of a room full of firelight. A bed hung with red curtains occupied the centre with an undraped woman's figure of the loveliest lines, getting into it: one ivory knee pressed the side of the bed: her fair hair, glinting with red in the firelight, fell over her shoulders and her rounded arm, uplifted to draw aside the curtain. Underneath the picture was written the one word, "RUBY."

George Morris, city man, living in the suburbs with Mrs. Morris in the dull, solid round of English existence, felt his heart leap up suddenly in response to the call of the picture. Under a plain, prosaic exterior this man had a deep natural love for romance, a thirst for adventure, a longing for the "wine, woman and song" that seemed never to form a part of his humdrum life. He thought of Mrs. Morris and her dull, plain face and the ginger-brown gown she seemed to live in. Why did she always wear brown, he wondered? Why not red, for instance? He thought of their bedroom at Meadow View, Mervyn Road: its linoleum floor, its iron bedstead, its white walls, its narrow grate filled with tissue paper and never guilty of a fire. In fact, it was always so cold that Maria Morris wore very thick nightgowns and woolly jackets to keep warm, and the electric light was so expensive now that she would hardly allow it to be used upstairs, and always said they could just as well undress in the dark.

George sighed. Why was Maria like that and his bedroom like that? Why should he not have a rich, warm, red room like this ... and ... and...?

"There you are, sir: the best three-ply there is for picture backing."

George turned round with a start. He had quite forgotten his errand.

The dealer was peering at him through his spectacles, the thin wood in his hand.

"Er—ah!—thank you very much," he stammered. "Er—this picture here—what price is it?" He indicated the little red sketch.

"Oh, that's not for sale," replied the man. "It's just a bit an artist brought in to show me. He's painting quite a big picture. It's for the Salon, I believe."

"Oh," murmured George, "not for the Academy?" He felt disappointed he couldn't buy the sketch, and if the picture was going to Paris he would never see it again.

The dealer shook his head doubtfully. "No. I think not. Colour's a bit too warm for England, I should say."

The door bell sprang at the moment, and the dealer looked round a pile of frames into the front shop.

"Why, here is Mr. Brookes himself!" he exclaimed. And George saw a tall slight young man with the artist's slouch-hat and a flowing tie come in and nod to the shopman. "There's a gentleman here admiring your picture," the latter said, and George approached him eagerly.

"I do indeed," he said. "It's a wonderful picture. I'm sorry I won't ever see the big one."

The artist flushed with pleasure. "You can come and see it now, if you like," he said in a pleased tone. "My shanty's only a stone's throw from here; two tubes of purple madder, please, Smith, and chalk them up, will you? I haven't a cent on me."

George's heart beat. A visit to a real studio with an artist to see this glorious red picture! He accepted at once. What a comfort that Maria had always been out to tea lately and there was no need for him to hurry back.

When the artist had got his paints and George had paid for his purchase, they left the shop together and walked to the studio.

It was in a side street, and you went down a long slope from the pavement to a wooden door which the artist opened with his latchkey, and George walked through a small passage into a great, untidy, comfortable room that, with its hint of gaiety and dissolute romance, delighted him. There were deep chairs everywhere, a huge dais in one corner all draped in gorgeous red, a stove in the centre glowing hot, a deep cushioned semi-circular lounge half round it. One corner of the room was walled off with voluminous blue curtains to form the artist's bedroom. The whole end of the room farthest from this was window, but it only looked into a quiet green garden with high walls round affording complete seclusion. There was a delightful litter of pictures all about, a mass of flowers by the sunny window, an aviary of singing birds, soft Turkey rugs on the floor, and the perfume of scented cigarettes in the air. George liked it. He liked it much better than the stiff drawing room with the starched white curtains and high hard chairs of Meadow View.

The artist drew forward two big chairs and then, going to the dais pulled on a cord. The curtains flew apart and there was the picture! Then he threw himself into one of the chairs while George took the other, and the two men gazed at the canvas in silence.

"Wonderful woman she is," remarked the artist after a minute between the puffs of his cigarette. "Bit of a mystery. Calls herself Mrs. Brown, but don't believe that's her real name. Can't make out what she's doing it for: whether it's the money or for the fun of it; little of both, perhaps. She's not a regular model evidently, but she's one of the best I ever had. Good figure, isn't it?"

"Oh, perfect, perfect!" replied George rapturously. He couldn't take his eyes off the picture. He sat before it spellbound, clasping his British umbrella in both hands as it stood between his British knees gazing at the vivid, barbaric riot of beautiful colour and suggestion that appealed so to his romantic un-British heart. "What's her face like?"

"Oh, nothing very much. Not a bad little face when she smiles and gets some colour; but you see I didn't want the face for that picture."

"No, quite so, quite so," assented George.

27

"Larky woman, I should think," went on the artist. "Married to a sort of dull brute of a husband—doesn't care about her; leaves her alone all day."

"Pig!" grunted George indignantly. "Can you imagine a man having a woman like that and neglecting her?"

The artist laughed.

"Well, marriage is a killing atmosphere. I don't know what she may be at home, she's amusing enough when she comes in here."

"What do you know about her? Where did you meet her?"

"The funny part is I don't know anything. She just walked in here one afternoon: said she was bored to death and had no romance or fun in her life, and no money of her own to spend. Said she'd sit as a model if I'd have her. I wasn't much struck at first: she was rather badly dressed, you know; but we talked a little bit and I got rather interested. I'd had the idea for this picture for a long time, I hadn't a model, and she was cheap and very willing to learn and be civil, which all of them are not, and so there it was. She's been coming to me for quite a time now, and it's good, the picture, isn't it? I'm hoping it'll make a big hit."

George nodded. He was grasping his umbrella feverishly, his hands rolling and unrolling the silk flaps nervously. He would do it, he would. He'd have this one bit of romance in his life to cherish and look back upon.

He turned to the insouciant artist who, with his head tilted back and the cigarette in his teeth and his leg hanging over one arm of the chair, was contemplating his work with satisfaction through half-closed eyes.

"I think I heard you say in that shop you were a little pressed for ready money," he said in his rather stiff way.

The artist laughed. "Dead broke, my dear sir, that's what I am! Why? Are you thinking of making me an offer for the picture?"

George leant nearer him.

"The picture's good," he said hoarsely, for his throat felt dry, "but it's the woman I want. Do you want to make twenty pounds? Well, here's your chance. Get her for me. Get her here. Lend me the studio for a few hours. Fix up those red curtains, have it just like the picture, red lights, red fire, red roses, red everything. Get her posing just like that, mind, just like that; then you clear out and leave us alone."

The artist was sitting bolt upright now staring at Mr. George Morris as if he could not believe his eyes or his ears, as indeed he could not. Was this really the very respectable old party he had met in the shop? His eyes were glowing, his face flushed. He looked almost young and handsome. What an astounding proposition from such an orthodox-looking old Briton! Still, twenty pounds....

"But I don't suppose for one minute she'd consent," he said after an astonished pause of reflection.

George made an angry movement of impatience.

"Unless you muddle things," he said, "she won't know anything about it. You won't ask her anything."

"But I don't see...." began the other.

"Look here. You get the lady to come to an ordinary sitting; just as usual. You fix up everything, just as it is there, as you always do, I suppose. I'm waiting behind those curtains there. Then you get her to pose just like that: you step back to

28

get something, brush or what-not. You slip behind the curtains and then clear out of the studio and I am left in your place. What's to prevent you doing that?"

"Nothing. Only it seems rather a bad trick for me to play her and she may disappoint you, she may...."

"Never mind," returned George calmly now. "If I muddle my own affairs when you leave us that's my business; nothing to do with you. You get your twenty all the same."

"When?" asked the artist dubiously.

"When I look through those curtains," returned George intimating the artist's walled-off bedroom behind them, "and see this picture in life. When you pass me to go out I'll slip the notes into your hand."

Mr. James Brookes looked down on the floor in silent thought. He didn't like the idea at all. Still, he was very hard up and perhaps his model would not mind. She seemed very good natured. He could pass it off as a practical joke.

"I don't half like it," he said after a minute. "Still, I'll do it."

"When?"

"Day after to-morrow she's coming—four to six. You'd better be here by three-thirty, so there's no chance of her seeing you come in."

George got up with a strange fire of joy in his heart. Here was romance, intrigue, adventure, coming into his life at last!

He cast his eyes round the studio with its inviting air of ease, its bright colours, its luxury, which seemed to belie, or was it the cause of its owner's poverty?

"I envy you your life," he said, buttoning up his coat and gazing at the innumerable portraits of brunettes and blondes on the studio walls. "There must be so much beauty, poetry, colour in it, novelty, change." And he sighed, thinking of his eighteen years at Meadow View with Maria.

"Oh, I don't know," returned the artist. "One gets sick of it, you know; so many women and all jealous and squabbling with one another. One longs sometimes for a home and a little peace and quietness."

"What a pity we can't change places," mused George as he walked home thinking over the artist's words. Then he fell to wondering what the model's face would be like. "A nice little face when she smiles and gets some colour," the artist had said, and it rather took his fancy. Ruby! It was a sweet name! And she, like himself, was sighing for romance in her life, was evidently just as lonely and unappreciated as he was. By the time he got back to Mervyn Road, his face had assumed its usual chastened expression.

Maria seemed rather more dull and sour than usual.

"Why didn't you come back to tea?" she enquired.

George flushed.

"You have been out so often to tea lately," he said.

"Well, I wasn't to-day," she snapped. "You might let me know when you're not coming home till dinner."

"I'll be at the office late, I know, the day after to-morrow," replied George, trying to speak naturally, but getting redder and redder.

"All right," returned Maria, "I'm glad to know it. I'll go and have tea with Aunt Emma."

"Do, my dear, and I'll get back in time for dinner."

"I should hope so," rejoined Maria.

George was amiability itself that evening. The glow of the picture had got into his heart and warmed it, and that night he could not sleep for thinking of it. What might not this adventure lead up to? He had heard of men who had cosy little flats, the existence of which was unknown to their lawful wives. He had always thought this very wrong, but now he began to feel sympathy with those men. Perhaps, like himself they had dull, unsympathetic wives; perhaps they, too, were yearning after colour in their lives. A little flat and all furnished in red, which could be kept very warm so that its occupant could wear those nice pink and blue things he saw in the windows of the Burlington Arcade, and dispense with woolly jackets. Silk stockings, too! He had often thought it would be nice to have someone to take those neat boxes of silk stockings home to that he saw on the counter of men's shops when he went to buy his ties. He had never thought of Maria. Silk stockings didn't go with Meadow View—they went with little flats. Of course, it might be rather expensive, but then, why should he not spend something on his own amusements? He was very liberal with Maria. She was always buying new hats. Now last year, she had had—how many? There was the hat with the green feathers, and—er—er the hat with the green feathers, and—and—the hat with the green feathers. Well, there, he couldn't think of any other hat, so he supposed she had had only one last year, and finally, trying to find another hat for Maria, he fell asleep.

*   *   *   *   *

The great day came and with a beating heart, Mr. George Morris left his office early and hurried to the studio, arriving there some minutes before the appointed time. The artist let him in himself, and George thought the studio looked more attractive than ever. The sun was streaming through the lowered red blinds, the stove was burning brightly, there were flowers on the many little tables and a heavy fragrance from burning pastilles in the air. He was quite sorry to have to go into the dark recesses of the bedroom in the corner, but his host insisted on it and gave him a chair well back against the wall away from the curtain. He gave him a paper, but as it was too dark to read there with any comfort and he was strictly enjoined not to make the faintest noise, so that he could not turn its pages, it was obvious the paper was not much use to him. And how could anyone read in that state of high-strung expectation in which Mr. George Morris now found himself?

After sitting there alone in the obscurity for what seemed an interminable time, he heard a ring at the main door and the artist going out to answer it. They seemed to linger a long time at the door and he thought he heard some ripples of laughter that set all his pulses beating. Then he heard the studio door open and evidently two persons entering. But he was disappointed that he could not hear their conversation, hardly their voices through the muffling folds of the heavy curtains. He was afraid to leave his seat and approach nearer the curtains for fear lest some noise of his movement might betray him. The model's ears might be sharper than his own. There was quite a long pause of silence, and he wondered what they were doing. Perhaps the model was undressing. Then he heard the moving of furniture and supposed the scene was being arranged. The heavy bed with its elaborate red drapery that figured in the picture had to be pushed to its right position on the dais. He sat impatiently on his chair, the notes all ready in his hand to be given to the artist in that blissful moment when he should pass by him on his way out, leaving him alone with the adorable model.

At last his host's light step approached the other side of the curtains, a hand was laid on them, and he heard his voice say: "I'll just fetch that tube," and then the curtains were pulled apart.

Morris sprang to his feet and stood spellbound. There was the lovely picture in the life, the warm interior, the gorgeous bed, the crimson lights and in the centre, the feminine figure of lovely whiteness with the flowing hair in the pose of just getting into bed.

The artist passed swiftly by him, pulled the notes out of George's nerveless hand as he stood there staring, then passed on noiselessly to the door which he closed behind him with the faintest click. Faint though it was, it came to George's ears and roused him. He was alone—the room, the scene, the model was his! With outstretched arm he rushed forward to clasp this beauty, this dream, this delight to him. He reached the dais. His arms were almost round her lovely shoulders when the model turned.

A shriek rang through the studio: "*George!*"

"*Maria!*"

31

A NOVEL ELOPEMENT

The train puffed its way along its line through one of the prettiest parts of Kent and carried among its many passengers a bridal couple that had that morning been married and were now *en route* for their honeymoon.

Three weeks ago they had never seen each other, these two, who now at the respective ages of eighteen and twenty-five, had taken their solemn oath to remain together till Death. They had met at a dance. He had been in the mood to marry somebody; she was already rather tired of refusing offers and accepted his for a change. Their engagement had been a joyous whirl, and both were very happy now and were quite convinced that their choice was excellent. Eva thought Eric was so clever and had such a wonderful mind and character because he always agreed with her in conversation. Eric was so occupied with gazing into her blue eyes when he answered her searching questions, that he had not the remotest idea what it was he agreed to. If she said she loved dogs he said he thought there was nothing so jolly and faithful; if she said women should have votes, he said it would be a shame if they hadn't. If she said she adored music, he said his happiest hours were passed listening to her playing; if she said vivisection was a blot on our civilization, he said it was a beastly, unnatural practice and ought to be stopped. If she said the traffic in old horses should be abolished he told her his idea had always been to found a home where old horses could end their days in peace. Once, when he trod on the tail of her mother's cat, he had seemed, to her surprise, a little callous about it. She had reproached him. The cat had been picked up immediately by him, fondled on his knee and given a saucer of milk by way of consolation.

Eva simply glowed with joy and love after such conversations and incidents, and when her mother pointed out that she knew very little of the man and that the engagement was very short, she answered:

"It doesn't matter, we are so alike and take the same view of everything. We are sure to be happy."

She honestly thought she saw him in his words. All she saw was what he let her see—the reflection of her own warm-hearted, clear-headed self. She had really thought out the subjects on which she formed her well-founded opinions. When she offered these to him, as he never thought out anything and had no opinions, he accepted hers just as lightly and easily as he would have accepted the contrary ones, if offered!

It is always very difficult for the deep, strong nature of a woman to realise the facile worthlessness of a man's. She was happy as she sat in the corner of the carriage, her hand tucked into his. She was sure—or *nearly* sure—that she had found a good, great man. He was quite sure he had found a girl with a pretty face and nice figure—these were clear to the eye, no bother of thinking them out—so both young people were blissfully content and satisfied.

Suddenly the easy motion of the train stopped. A jar and a jerk, then it drew up motionless where the line ran through a pretty wood. Eric sprang up and put his head out of the window. It was autumn, the evening chill, and dusk. He could not see ahead—only that they were not stopping at any station. Presently the guard came along by the side of the train:

"There's an obstruction on the line, sir, on ahead! Part of a tunnel fallen in. It will take some clearing away, too. We can't get on to-night."

Most of the other passengers were looking out and listening to his discouraging accents. Their eyes wandered over the wood in which the train was pulled up. It stood golden in autumn leaf, silent and chill. It seemed unresponsive, and to offer no solution of their difficulties. Then plans began to be made and eagerly discussed. Some of the passengers were in favor of returning to the last station and stopping there the night, being somewhat reluctantly assured by the guard they could "get on in the morning."

Eric withdrew his head and sat down by Eva.

"What would you like to do, darling?"

Eva was gazing into the mystery of the shadowy wood.

"Could we camp there?" she said. "Under that golden canopy, it's very lovely!"

Eric's face lengthened.

"Hardly, dear, I think. It's so damp and——"

"There is a lovely full moon rising behind the trees," she answered.

Eric was silent. The wood did not appeal to him, nor the rising moon. Neither did the "Bull and Cow" which was the station inn and the only one they had seen from the last station as they passed.

In the pause that ensued the guard entered the carriage and approached the young couple confidentially.

"We've decided to make a run back, sir, from here; but if I may make a suggestion, there's a nice farmhouse not a stone's throw from here where you'd be most comfortable. I know the party as keeps it would put you up for the night and give you a good supper."

Eva looked up brightly.

"A farmhouse? Is it a pretty one?"

"Well, I couldn't say as it's so very pretty," returned the guard doubtfully, "but there's good ale to be had and fowls and pork and nice rooms, too, what they let in the summer."

Eric became decisive.

"I think, darling, that's really the best we can do, and if it's quite near we can get our light luggage carried over."

A man was found by the guard. They gathered their wraps and light cases together. In a few moments they were standing on the damp soil by the side of the train, listening to the directions he was giving for the route.

It did not sound so very near:

"You keeps away from the wood and you goes up the hill to the top and then down on the other side till you comes to the bridge, and don't cross the bridge, but keep along by the stream till you get to a stile, and you cross the stile and go through two fields and then there's a bit of a wood and you go through the wood and then you comes out on a bit of a slope and the farm's just facing you."

"But that's a long way," expostulated Eric. Eva was surprised at his cross tone. She had never heard it before.

"It will be a lovely walk on this moonlight night," she volunteered.

"It's not more'n fifteen minutes or 'arf-an-hour's walk," said the guard in an aggrieved tone, "and you can't miss it, and the ale's good."

Eric tipped him. The man shouldered the cases and they started. They followed their instructions to keep away from the wood and took a little narrow path that wound up to the top of the hill. The moon was just peeping over its brow and made long shadows fall from the trees that stood here and there. The air was damp and cool and full of the scent of late roses and wet leaves.

To the girl it was all pure enjoyment, only clouded a little by the fact that Eric seemed so put out. They walked side by side in silence. The man trudged along behind them, silent also. Up and up till the ridge was reached, then down and down on the other side. Eva walked with springing steps admiring the calm beauty of it all, drawing pleasure from each little detail of star in the sky or gleam of moonlight on the brook. She hazarded a few enthusiastic remarks, but Eric did not seem to hear them, and there was silence until the second field beyond the stile was reached. Then through the quiet air came suddenly to them a strange sound—a low, hollow sound of misery. Eva stopped:

"What is that sound, Eric?"

"Dog barking, I should think," he answered shortly.

"I never heard a dog bark like that before; it has an awful, extraordinary sound."

"Yes, because the beast has barked himself hoarse, I should think, that's all."

Eva stood listening.

"Yes, I suppose it is hoarse as you say, but what a terrible sound."

It was a terrible lamenting cry of a soul in misery that came to them wailing over the wood and the stream.

"Please come along," Eric said as she stood there with dilating eyes. "We don't want to spend the night here."

Eva walked on. The sound of the barking, if barking it could be called, becoming clearer and nearer as they advanced. They were in the wood now, and the moonlight falling through the trees made beautiful patterns and traceries on the moss-grown path, but Eva now had no eyes for it. She was listening to that long-drawn wail of pain that came fitfully through the silver air.

"But aren't you sorry for it?" she asked.

"I don't know. It's barked itself into that condition, I expect. I suppose it's one of the farm dogs. I hope the brute won't go on like that all night."

Eva was silent. It was not quite what she expected Eric to say, but she made no comment.

34

They were through the wood, on the slope, and there was the farmhouse at last facing them on the slope opposite.

It looked comfortable enough and cheery; well-built and solid with a warm blaze of light in its lower windows. A large farmyard was close at its side; an orchard on the other side. From behind the house the hollow, melancholy barking continued, belying the aspect of peace and rest.

At the door of the farmhouse they received a warm welcome. It was thrown open by the stout, good-tempered looking woman herself, while her husband and son, burly figures in their rough farm clothes, lounged up to the threshold, hands in pockets, to stare at the strangers. Behind them at the end of the passage or hall a door stood open to warmth and lights and a table laid for supper.

Farmer Bates and his wife let rooms in the summer, so they knew the ways of the rich and those who were not farmers. There was no difficulty. They could have a nice room, they could have hot water, they could have baths and they could have early tea in the morning; they could have roast chicken and soup and apple tart for supper.

Eric cheered up and Eva saw the expression she was familiar with come back to his face. The "engagement expression" as she now christened it in her mind. It was the only one she had seen for those three weeks—the only one she knew— but she saw now his face had others.

She was asked to go in and sit by the fire, and did so while the farmer's young, handsome son took the place opposite. Eric was arranging terms with the woman and seeing their luggage carried upstairs.

The young farmer started a conversation as he was accustomed to do with the summer visitors. Eva was preoccupied; she wanted to ask about the dog, but she hesitated as to how best to approach the subject, and before she had decided, the others came back into the room.

The supper was quite a merry meal for all except herself. It was all quiet outside now, but in spite of the talk going on round her, her ears were only listening for that call from without. Eric grew quite jovial; he approved the farmer's ale and drank heartily. The farming family were pleased at their guests' appreciation, and the prospect of the good pay coming in. Bridegrooms were always generous. Suddenly, across the laughter and the talk, it came again; that awful wail of hopeless misery. The hosts did not appear to hear it, but Eva's face blanched, and a look of annoyance flashed across Eric's handsome countenance.

Eva turned to the young man next her:

"Why has that dog got such a peculiar bark?" she asked.

"Because he's going mad, I think," he answered. "We're going to shoot him in the morning."

The young farmer was quite surprised by the look of distress that come to the girl's face.

"Oh, but why?" she exclaimed. "I think from his bark he wants water. Let me take him some."

The man laughed:

"You take him water? Why you couldn't get near him. He's so savage he'd eat you alive."

"What has made him so savage?"

"Well, we've kept him on the chain for seven years, and it's sent him crazy, I think," he answered indifferently. "We haven't been able to get near him for years; we just throw him his food and push the water to him with a pole."

"Do you mean you've kept him chained up and never let him free once, never given him any exercise for seven years?"

"Oh, he gets exercise enough dancing about at the end of that chain and howling. We let him howl in the winter for we don't notice him, and it's too much trouble to go out and bash him, but in the summer when the visitors are here we thrash him when he barks, for they don't like it, and if it annoys you I'll soon settle him now."

And before she realised what he was going to do, he rose from his place, strode up to where some huge horsewhips were ranged against the wall, and then with one in his hand, went to the door. The burly farmer turned in his chair.

"That's right, Steve, you go and give him a good hiding. Teach him to behave when we have ladies here."

The son would have gone out, but Eva had sprung up and she put herself between him and the door.

"Pray don't," she said. "It does distress me to hear him, but I wouldn't have him beaten for anything."

The young farmer looked down into her blanched face and dilated eyes. Their beauty conquered him.

"As you like," he said rather sullenly, and hung the whip up again on the wall.

The farmer himself laughed.

"Now then, missis," he called banteringly. "You've no call to interfere. If he wants to beat our dog, why shouldn't we?"

"Don't be foolish, Eva. Come and sit down," Eric said. His tone was full of annoyance.

She came back to the table and sat down facing the farmer. She was white and trembling.

"It's not your dog," she said steadily.

The farmer's red face turned purple.

"Not our dog, eh! Not our dog! And 'oos dog is it, then, I should like to know?"

"It's God's dog," the girl replied unflinchingly.

She had a beautiful voice, very soft and sweet in tone, but full of power. It vibrated through the room now, charged with the intensity of her feelings and held her listeners:

"All animals are His. He created them. They are not ours. They are only lent to us in trust, and it is *my* business to interfere, as it is everybody's business to interfere when they are ill-treated and mis-used."

No one spoke for a moment. The farmer sat back, open-mouthed.

"'Pon my word," he stuttered after a minute. "'Pon my word," and could get no further.

They all turned instinctively to Eric to see what view he would take, and Eva, too, looked at him appealingly. Surely he would take her side against the others!

"Eric?" she said questioningly. He coloured hotly. He was annoyed at her making a scene like this about nothing.

"Don't be stupid, Eva," he said shortly. "Go on with your supper. Of course Bates has a right to do as he thinks best. Personally, I think it would be a good thing if he did give the brute a thrashing and stopped his howling."

"Eric!" she exclaimed again, but this time her tone was one of sheer amazement and bewilderment, and sitting in her place she stared across at him as if he were some new strange monster suddenly presented to her eyes. And indeed, this was the fact. She saw, for the first time, the real Eric. This was not the man she had married this morning, surely? This was not the man whose eyes had been wont to fill with sympathetic tears whenever she had wept. A feeling of extreme loneliness came over her. He was one in spirit with these coarse-faced, brutal farmers, who had tortured their four-footed servant for seven years and thrashed him when he had cried to them for help.

She was alone amongst them all.

She had no husband. That man opposite her, who had just let fall those words, was not the one she had loved and adored and married. By his speech he seemed to have let loose an icy river which was flowing now wide and deep as the Polar sea between them.

"Don't sit staring at me," Eric said impatiently. "Go on with your supper, for Heaven's sake."

Eva's lips set. She pushed her plate from her and rose.

"Thank you, I have finished," she merely said, but there was such a cutting disdain in her voice, such a thin, frosty edge to her tone, that it seemed to those at the table a shower of ice had fallen suddenly upon them. She stood for a moment looking down on the circle, at the flushed, bloated faces, at the burly lounging forms of these men who could sit there stuffing themselves to their protruding eyes; well-warmed, well-fed, well-clothed, and knowing that their faithful friend and devoted defender was stretched on the cold stones a few feet away, dying in the agonies of thirst and despair.

She turned and left the room before anyone moved or spoke, and went upstairs to the bedroom.

She opened the door. A fire had been lighted in the grate, and its cheerful red light was playing all over the room. The blinds were pulled down, and thick red curtains drawn across the windows. On the neat dressing-table stood a vase full of dried lavender. The bed in the corner with snowy sheets and counterpane invited to repose. Another little bed, draped in pink dimity, stood near the window.

It was a room in which any weary traveller would have liked to rest.

Eva noticed nothing. She shut the door behind her, then walked over to the window, pulled aside the curtains and let the spring blind fly up with a snap. Then she looked out, and there was the dog! Facing her across a large stone paved yard, fully illuminated by the brilliant moonlight so that she could see every detail. At the extreme end of his chain, his long-nailed paws on the stone flags, the wild-eyed, dishevelled looking creature stood, gazing towards the house where his tormentors lived. The girl's quick eyes took in his gaunt and bony frame, the rough hair that stood upright down his spine, the open jaw with white foam hanging from it, the neck from which all the hair was gone, rubbed away in his ceaseless efforts to free himself from his chain. Near him were a few bones and untouched scraps. Just out of his reach, however he might strain, was an overturned earthenware saucer. It looked dry, as if it had not contained water for many days.

So little like a dog the creature looked, she could not determine to what breed it belonged, but it seemed to have been something between a mastiff and a wolfhound. Now it was just a huge, wasted wreck, glaring-eyed, demented, that man had made.

And she looked out at it and pitied it and loved it with that boundless love and sympathy for all suffering things, that is the best part of the female nature.

So he had stood in that stone-paved yard, week in week out for seven years— day after day, night after night, of burning sun and intolerable heat, or icy cold and cutting winds. No shelter, not even a kennel, not even a trace of straw. All round him was a ring of shining white on the grey flags which his scratching feet had made in his hopeless efforts to be free; and the physical sufferings were the least of what he had borne. The worst had been the awful monotony of those long, dreary days without hope, without aim or occupation: that emptiness and that sameness that preys on an animal's brain just as much as on a man's.

Chained up in his youthful days, with all the wild longings for the twenty-mile run, the smell of the wildwoods, the finding of mates, fermenting in his blood, with his great canine heart full of that wonderful enthusiastic worship of man that Nature has planted there, longing for love and companionship, for the touch of a kind hand on his head, he had watched the homestead with wistful, hungering eyes. And because, when people approached him, he had tugged so frantically at his chain and pawed the air to show his joy and longing to follow them, he had been thought savage, and when he had cried out in his loneliness, he had been beaten into quietude; but his agony and his sorrow, and his wonder at it all was so great that even those cruel thrashings had not silenced him.

And now, after seven years of this, he was to be shot to-morrow! The girl, looking out at him, understood all he had gone through, and a fierce resentment against his tormentors rose and swelled within her like a great wave. Somehow, she would save him, she determined, and give him a little happiness before he died; give him that love and sympathy his heart had been craving for all those years. She had forgotten herself, forgotten it was her wedding evening—a time so passionately anticipated during her engagement. As for Eric, he seemed to have disappeared from her. Somewhere between the Church and the farmhouse the Eric she loved had vanished. How could she reach that poor, condemned prisoner? If she went down now to the farmhouse door she would be heard unfastening it, even if she could move those solid bars. If she were seen in the yard she would certainly be followed and prevented from getting near the dog. No one else could be persuaded to release him. Everyone was afraid of those gleaming teeth and blood-shot eyes. She would only probably succeed in getting him shot that night instead of to-morrow. And how would they shoot him? Not with one merciful bullet sent direct to the brain; but probably aiming from a distance, they might shoot and wound him a dozen times and then perhaps leave him dying and not dead.

They would certainly kill him in the same clumsy, misunderstanding way they had treated him while alive. Merely to release him in his present condition, wild-looking and supposed to be mad, would be no kindness. If he dashed away he would soon be followed, perhaps stoned by the screaming rabble of the village. No, she must not only release him, she must take him away and with her. He was her dog now. No one wanted him. He was going to be shot. Well, she would not have that. She would take him. Then suddenly she remembered Eric. He would certainly object! and she was married. She had to consult him.

She turned from the window in a sudden panic—she was a prisoner, too. And her gaoler was of the stamp of the men downstairs. How awful this was! She had never meant to marry such a man. Had he shown himself before the ceremony as he had at the supper here, she would never have married him. Her hands turned cold, and her knees shook. She sank down in a chair by the fire. She had never realized the prison side of marriage.

Union with the twin soul she had thought she had found in Eric had not suggested it. But now she saw how the case was. Had she been travelling alone she could have gone to the farmer and paid him his own price for the dog and taken him away with her, openly. It would have been quite simple. But now she knew instinctively Eric would not let her do this and as he was against her as well as all those downstairs, the dog would probably be shot before her eyes and she would be powerless to prevent it because she had given up her single freedom of action, given up the right over her own conduct. And to that man! It was horrible. Her nails sank into her clenched hands. In that moment she longed to be free of that room, free of her marriage as the dog outside longed to be free of his chain. The sex passion is infinitely curious in its nature. Though in some ways so strong, so resistless, yet in others it is so frail a plant that the lightest wind may sweep it away. Eva had given to Eric not only love and admiration, but also the natural joyous passion of awakened girlhood. Now all these were equally dead. She sat there, numb and cold with only one desire—to save the dog and escape.

As she sat trying to think out some plan of action, the door opened and Eric came in. The supper had done him good; his bad temper was forgotten. He came in smiling, and she saw again the old Eric with the "engagement expression." Suddenly it occurred to her she could win her way by blandishment however her feelings might have changed. For the dog's sake she must dissemble and act.

She went up to him with arms outstretched.

"Oh, Eric darling, I am so glad you have come. Do do me a favor, and I'll simply adore you. Do let us buy that poor dog and take him away with us and make up to him for all he has suffered."

The smile died away from the man's face. He unclasped her arms from his neck.

"But, my dear child, he's mad. You can't take a mad dog about with you. His own people are afraid to go near him."

"I should think they would be after the way they have treated him," she answered with burning indignation. "But *I'm* not afraid of him. He is not mad. He is only crazy with loneliness and thirst. Let me go down and release him, and I'll be responsible for him."

Eric stared at her in amazement and with a growing anger fed by jealousy and wounded vanity.

A man's nerves and state of general self-control are not at their best on such an occasion as this, and in his unbalanced condition it seemed intolerable to him that his bride should not be wholly occupied with himself but should be worrying over a miserable brute of a dog. It did not occur to him that she was only now displaying those qualities that had so much attracted him from the first—that soft, warm heart, that all-embracing love and sympathy that coupled with her physical beauty had made him decide to marry her out of all the women he might have chosen. It did not occur to him either what a priceless possession of adoring love he might have gained for all the rest of his life by yielding to her then and conquering himself; nor how, for ever he would kill his own future by opposition. He was simply intensely angry, jealous and annoyed and blinded by hurt vanity and selfish passion.

"It's our *duty* to do something," she urged. "Come and look at him," and she drew him, reluctant, to the window.

The dog stood in the same position at the end of the hateful chain! his eyes glaring, his mouth open, his body shivering. The man and woman looked out at him together. The woman's eyes saw a fellow creature's suffering soul, the man saw—a mad dog.

"It's really nothing whatever to do with us," he expostulated, "it's not our business. The people who own him must know how to manage him. Why do you bother yourself about it!"

Eva turned and gazed at him with sheer surprise.

"But Eric, we couldn't possibly enjoy ourselves and sleep comfortably up here knowing he is there in such misery!"

"Of course, we could, if you were not so silly about it," he answered.

Eva was silent. Power to reply seemed taken away from her in face of this colossal adamantine hardness. She began to realise that this man she had married was not at all the exceptional individual she had imagined, but just the ordinary usual human being, not actively cruel, but absolutely indifferent and callous, not caring about anything except the satisfaction of his senses and the comfort of his own body.

"Well, if you could, I couldn't," she said after a moment. "Let me go down and unchain him and tell the people I'll buy him. If you don't want him with us, I'll send him to my sister to keep for me."

"To attempt to unchain a dog in that condition is going to your death," he said shortly, keeping control over himself as well as he could.

"I am sure it's not so, but even if it were and I feel it's my duty, I ought to do it. Why, Eric, how many times in the War did you not go forward to almost certain death just because it was your duty?"

Eric coloured furiously.

"That may be, but I'm not going to risk my life now to free a mad dog."

"I'm not asking you to. I want to free him."

"And my answer is, you shan't do anything so damnably foolish." Swept by a sudden whirl of anger that was utterly beyond him to control, he strode across the room, locked the door, tore out the key and flung it with all his force through the window. It fell tinkling on the stone flags of the yard.

"Now that ends all this damned nonsense," he said violently, and drew her roughly away from the window which he closed, and pulled the curtain across.

The girl stood as if turned into stone. As the key fell, a cry escaped her. A cry so bitter with hate and loathing that he might well have shuddered if he had noted it. But he did not. He did not realise it was the death-cry of the last shred of love or feeling of allegiance to him that was left in her heart.

The explosion of rage had helped Eric to become normal again. Having now secured, as he supposed, beyond all possibility of doubt, his own way, he became calmer. The brain-storm passed. He came up to where she stood, mute and motionless by the hearth.

"Darling," he said, attempting to draw her into his arms, "don't be stupid and spoil all our pleasure. Have you forgotten how we looked forward to being like this alone together?"

She wrenched herself away from him, and there was such a fury of resentment in her eyes that even he fell back from her with a confused sense of having made some fatal error. Women were intended by Nature to rule the world, not men, and that is why any attempt to coerce a woman by man generally fails.

"Don't touch me," she said in a voice low and sharp with the intensity of her anger. "You shall never touch me again."

"You seem to forget you're my wife," he said hotly.

"If I am fifty thousand times your wife I will never give myself to you. You can kill me first."

Eric stepped back and regarded her with dismay. He was face to face now with a force which he could only dimly comprehend. But as the storm had passed from his brain, it had left his intellect fairly clear, and he began to see things were getting serious. Somehow he was making a mess of it. Mechanically he turned away, fumbling in his pocket for his cigarette case. He drew out a cigarette, lighted it and began to smoke. What would be best to do, he wondered. Perhaps, if he said nothing she would calm down again. He rather wished he had not been so hasty. He wished he had put the key in his pocket instead of throwing it out of the window. There was no getting out of the room now for either of them. He regretted he had not been wiser and temporised more.

Presently he threw himself into a chair, and watched her furtively. Her eyes were turned away towards the fire. She stood like a thing turned into stone.

"What are we going to do, then?" he said, half banteringly, when the silence became unbearable. "Sit up all night?"

"As you please," the girl replied, without turning her head. He wondered what she was thinking about, and debated feverishly with himself what he should do or say. He would have been astonished if he could have known her thoughts. He had not the faintest conception of the character and the will he was dealing with.

The girl stood there,—Herself, sunk utterly in her thought. How to gain her end and carry out the dog's deliverance was the only thing that occupied her. Eric's last words had suddenly flashed a light into her brain. For a moment, when the key had whizzed by her and clinked on the stones without, hope had died in her. It seemed so impossible then to ever reach the poor chained one down there in time, but now his words, "sit up all night" showed her suddenly the contrary proposition. If Eric were once asleep and she, alone awake in the room, she could effect her escape from it by the window. Her heart gave a suffocating leap upward as the whole plan unrolled itself like a map before her mental vision. Light and agile as a cat, it would be possible for her to swing herself down by knotted sheets to the yard, loose the prisoner, and with him run through the moon-lighted country, back to that station down the line their train had passed, and catch the first one back to London. It was all most dangerous and difficult, most open to failure, still it was a *possible* plan—if Eric were asleep.

And with an infinite sense of horror and loathing, she realised the best and perhaps the only way to ensure his sleep was to reverse all she had said, to humiliate herself, to act a part, to give herself to him—and let him sleep. She saw his plan now was to sit up and smoke waiting and hoping she would change her mind. Time was passing, and each silver minute of the night brought the prisoner outside nearer to his doom.

She suddenly bent her head down on the mantelpiece. Nothing she would hate so much now as the caress of this man in whose caresses she had once so rejoiced! These moments she had so looked forward to, how horrible, how terrible they were now! His embrace! Surely with that fury of resentment in her heart, she would suffocate in it! But the dog had to be saved, and to accomplish that she would go through any suffering, any degradation. She drew herself together with a supreme effort of will, and turned to the man in the chair.

"Eric, I am so sorry I spoke as I did. Let's never mind about anything. Let's forget it. Kiss me."

He had sprung to his feet at her first word. She was beside him now, looking up at him with her glorious eyes full of light and her face glowing with smiles, though her heart was shuddering within her.

"Darling, my own, I am so sorry too," Eric was covering her upturned face with kisses. "My dearest, my very own."

Outside, the dog stood cold and stiff in the damp night air, aching with thirst, his poor, half-crazy eyes turned up to the moonlit sky from which no mercy came. The hours crept by, till the clock in the village struck three. For seven years he had listened to those strokes that marked the passing hours, hours that never brought him nearer to liberty, to the free use of his cramped limbs, to any of the natural joys for which he had been created. He sank wearily down on his haunches. He could no longer cry out; his voice seemed broken in his throat, his tongue was swollen and black. He kept his head turned to the window where he had seen the two figures stand looking at him. Some faint, dull hope had stirred in him that they might be thinking of him, that they might be coming to him to alleviate his misery and his torment of thirst. But no, the window had been shut and had gone dark.

Inside the room the strokes of the clock vibrated through the stillness, and Eva, lying open-eyed and filled with desperate impatience, slid noiselessly out of bed, and with soundless movements and feverish haste began to dress. Eric was asleep. Never in all her life had she prayed for anything so fervently as she did now that he might remain so. With infinite caution she crept about the room, making her toilet to the minutest detail. Within her all her personal self felt humiliated, outraged, seething with fury, but she would not think of herself, only of the work ahead to be done.

Hurry generally means noise. Therefore, filled with burning impatience as she was, she had to move slowly, regulating each movement and each tip-toe step. Once Eric moved and sighed, and she started in terror and stood motionless, but he did not awake, and with a thumping heart and trembling fingers she went on with her preparations. When she was fully dressed to her hat, and with her gloves and purse stowed away in her bodice, together with Eric's clasp-knife that he had left lying on the table, she approached the unoccupied bed standing in the corner by the window, and inch by inch drew the sheets from it. These alone would have been too short a length for her purpose even when knotted together at their extreme ends, but she took the counterpane as well, and all three end to end she judged would let her nearly to the ground. At their country place at home her father had shown her how to escape in case of fire, and she knew now exactly what to do. She knotted the corner of the sheet tightly round the little wooden post of the bed, and then there was the barrier of the window to be surmounted. She did not dare to draw back the curtains for fear of the rattle of their rings, but she lifted them slowly and silently to one side and then with both hands and infinite care, guided the spring blind up and looked out. Her heart gave a leap of boundless sympathy as she saw the great dog sitting at the end of his tightly-drawn chain, still gazing towards the window—his only hope—as he had been hours ago.

No Juliet felt more eager to join her Romeo than this girl did now to get to the suffering animal and soothe its pain. And of such natures is the Kingdom of Heaven. Such people are those who make this earth a little less like hell. Blind and curtain out of the way, it still remained to open the window without noise. Very, very softly with indrawn breath and shaking heart, she raised it half way, just enough to let her through. Then she paid out her long rope of knotted bedclothes, and looking out, she saw it reached to within about eight feet of the yard.

Then, as often before in the fire drill, she crept on to the window sill, twisted her feet well round the dangling cloths and gripped them hard in her little hands. Then down, down she swung her light weight and dropped at length noiselessly to the ground. The captive in the yard rose to his feet and lowered his head, staring at her fixedly, but he gave no sound. Some instinct seemed to tell him that all this strange proceeding had something to do with him.

The girl, once out of the room and away from the sleeping man she had sworn to love and honour and cleave to till death, felt such a rush of joyous elation that it seemed to give her wings. Quite half her work was successfully accomplished. She ran swift and silent as a shadow across the yard.

As he realised she was actually coming to him, the enormous dog tore at his chain, and as he could not advance he reared himself on his hind legs, his front pawing at the air, his eyes almost out of his head, his foaming jaws wide open. It was a fearsome sight, but the girl went on unflinchingly, straight up to the desperate animal. Tall as she was the dog stood as high as herself, and as she reached him his great bony, shaggy paws descended heavily on her shoulders, and she put both her arms out under them and clasped him to her warm, loving breast. And the animal enveloped in that marvelous electricity that flowed out from her, soothed and calmed instantly by that contact with true loving humanity which he had longed for all through his dreary life stood perfectly still, all his raging pulses calmed, all his tormenting pains dying away.

"Darling, be good now while I release you," she said in his ear, and gently let him slide to his four feet. Then she knelt down beside him and put her hands to his collar.

The dog understood perfectly she had come to release him. At last, at last he would be free, and he stood patient and still as a statue, only his whole frame quivered and thrilled with joy. He felt her little fingers trying desperately to undo the hateful collar. Eva's heart beat almost to choke her. Suppose, suppose she failed to get it undone. Seven years had solidified the leather almost into iron; the brass point that pierced the leather was embedded in and had become one almost with it.

Both were welded together under a thick coat of verdigris. Every nail on her fingers was broken before she gave up the hopeless task of unstrapping it. Then, keeping one hand on the dog's head, she felt in her bosom for the knife.

Because she understood him so perfectly, and that his loneliness and forsaken neglect had been the chief sorrow of his life, she knew just how to manage him. When she failed to undo the collar, he felt his heart die within him and had she moved away from him, his poor desperate brain would have given way. But she kept quite close to him and that told him that all hope was not lost, and nerved him to patience. The collar was loose for the hair had been rubbed and the neck wasted away which had filled it, and there was room for the knife-blade to pass under the leather.

"Hold still, now, don't move," she whispered in tense tones, and then sawed with all her strength, outwards on the collar.

It seemed incredibly hard, but the knife was sharp and leather must in the end yield to steel.

After minutes that seemed hours she cut it through, and with one great bound the dog leapt away from chain and collar. Free! Free in the moonlit night! Eva rose to her feet, and he came back to her, lowering his great body down to the earth on his fore-paws, and then springing to his full height to put them on her breast to show his rapture. Elated, joyous, but still in terror of being overtaken, Eva threw one rapid glance over the silent house and up to the window where her long white rope hung gleaming in the moonlight.

Then "Come," she said to the dog, and close, side by side, they raced out of the yard by the door just behind where he had been chained. A door that was never fastened for he had guarded it so faithfully and securely. Out of the yard and through the wasty farmyard adjoining, then over the low wall surrounding it, and they were out on the slope, tearing away like mad things to the shelter of the wood.

Here they continued to run, down the narrow, mossy path that Eric and she had come by, filled with such different feelings the evening before. Silent now, with all their strength given to speed, but with perfect union of intention, they steadied down to an even trot, the dog modifying his pace to the human being's. He knew that she had saved him, freed him, and he was now her faithful slave for life. No evil, no danger should come near her. No enemy could lay a finger on her as long as an atom of strength remained in him to defend her. He was hers and she was his till death.

At last they reached the spot where the train had pulled up the previous evening, and Eva, still hounded by the fear of pursuit, after a few minutes' rest, ran on steadily, taking a little path that passed beneath evergreens near the railway.

The station down the line was thirteen miles distant, yet such is the force of joy and the power of will and determination that the girl felt hardly fatigued when she saw the red and green lights ahead of her; and she walked into the booking office with a light and springing step as the yawning clerk opened it.

The next train to London, the first in the day to carry the mails, left in fifteen minutes. She took her ticket and a dog ticket, and went out on to the platform and sat down. She felt such happiness, such joy in her success, her accomplished plan, that nothing in her life had equalled it, and all sense of pain and tiredness were entirely drowned in it.

The dog was more distressed than she. He fell heavily at her feet as she sat down. He was footsore, his limbs ached and he was oh, so thirsty, but he minded nothing. He was content.

Eva had been afraid to wait to give him water, but she bent over him now, looking anxiously at his swollen, hanging tongue. He did not ask for anything, only looked up at her with great eyes from which the wildness was already dying away; for had he not felt a soft hand on his head and heard a kind voice in his ear?

She rose to seek water for him, and, stiff and sore though he was, he dragged himself to his feet to follow her. He could not bear her to move away from him.

There was a little tap of water standing out from the wall further down the platform, and stooping down, she turned it on and made a little bowl of her two small, pink-palmed hands for him to drink from. At first he seemed hardly able to swallow, nor get the water over his swollen tongue, but she waited patiently, and at last he drank easily and freely as long as she thought good for him. Then they walked back to the seat and she sat down and took his head on her knees and smoothed back the harsh, rough hair and looked deep into his eyes, and they talked together, as lovers do, in looks and silence.

At last the train arrived, and the guard of it came along, swinging his lantern. He stopped when he caught sight of her daintily-dressed figure, and the huge, rough wolfhound at her side. She turned to him, her hand on the carriage door.

"Can I take him in the carriage with me?" she asked.

The guard flashed his light over them.

"Yes, that'll be all right. The train's almost empty," he replied, eyeing the dog. He was not at all anxious to have the grim-looking beast shut up with him in his van.

"Not many people travels at this time of night," he added inquisitively, looking in at her after she was seated and the dog had dropped onto the floor of the carriage.

Eva made no response, and he turned away mumbling in a dissatisfied tone: "Runaways and eloping couples, thieves and such—them's wot travels at night."

Two or three minutes more of this anguished suspense and then the train started, gathered speed and they were away—safe. She leant over the dog with a joyous laugh. Oh, the relief of that moving train! Not Eric nor Bates, nor all the farm hands could overtake them now.

"He talked of eloping couples; that's just what we are, aren't we, darling?" And the dog beat his great, waving brush of a tail on the carriage floor for answer. She sat back in a corner, for the first time realising that she was very tired, but the joy at her heart glowed more fiercely every moment as the train rushed on its non-stop run to town. She had done it all; she had succeeded so admirably. She had saved the dog. She did not believe they could be separated now. If Bates sued her for stealing his dog she was ready to pay his full value which the farmer would probably prefer; and Eric? What would he do or say or think when he woke and found himself alone in the room where he had locked himself? Would he climb down the sheets as she had done? She wondered and laughed. But whatever he did he should never approach her again.

Arrived in town she went straight to her sister, a girl of twenty, widowed in the War, who had always strenuously disapproved of Eric. Brushing past the astonished footman in the hall, she ran upstairs and found the beautiful Linda still in bed. She sat up in astonishment as Eva and the great hound burst into the room.

"Linda, I've eloped!"

"Well, you *are* modern! You were only married yesterday!"

46

"I know," Eva answered, sitting down in a deep armchair, "but I found I hadn't married the man I meant to after all, but somebody else that I didn't like at all."

"We most of us do that," returned Linda, swinging two ivory feet out of bed and eyeing the dog:

"What a beautiful dog. What's he doing here?"

Few would have applied that adjective to the great creature stretched before her. But Linda saw through the devastation man had made to the original beauty given by Nature.

"He is the cause of everything. I eloped with *him*."

"What do you mean? Tell me everything, now, from the beginning," and Linda wrapped herself in a rose-hued gown and settled herself to listen. The dog stretched himself out on his side between them and fell asleep, worn out, not so much by the physical exertions as the conflicting emotions of the night.

Eva told all; shortly, incisively. Only once did she give rein to her feelings—when she had to tell how she had bought Eric's passivity and sleep—she sprang up with her hands clenched into knots.

"If I have a child by him, I'll kill it before it breathes!" she exclaimed. "What is the good of multiplying callous brutes like that?"

Linda listened attentively to the end. Then she rose and rang the bell.

"You poor thing, you must be quite worn out. What you want is breakfast first and then sleep."

"But did I do rightly? Do tell me what you think, Lin."

"Of course I think so, and I think you have made a good exchange. A dog will never disappoint you—never go back on you—never be unkind to you, never be unfaithful to you and a man will—always."

Eva sighed, leaning back and closing her eyes.

"It's so good to be back with you, Lin."

The maid brought in hot coffee, and a huge breakfast tray of delicious edibles, and the girls laughed and talked as they ate, and the dog who had had bones flung to him on the flags, had a pile of delicate curly slices of bacon on a hand-painted porcelain dish. After breakfast Linda insisted on Eva going to bed, and there in that soundless room the girl and dog slept away the morning hours.

In the afternoon Eric came, and Eva went down to see him in the library.

"What does all this mean?" he asked as she closed the door and stood facing him.

"I am not coming back to you. Linda has asked me to stay with her, and I have accepted."

"But you married me!"

"No, that's where you make the mistake. I married a dream man, a man of my own imagination, a man who was decent and kind and humane, quite different from you altogether."

Eric flushed a dull, angry red.

"You consummated the marriage with *me* anyhow; you won't deny that, I suppose?" he said.

A look of intense repulsion came over her face.

"For the dog's sake, I gave myself to you, though I *loathed* you," she answered in a low tone, full of repressed vehemence.

"For the dog's sake," repeated Eric, growing more and more bewildered and less and less able to solve the problem that woman always presents to man. "How? I don't understand."

"You had determined to sit up all night and prevent me going to him; if I had had any chloroform or any drug to put you to sleep I would have given it to you. I had nothing but myself so I gave you that."

She was standing close to him and looking straight into his eyes. The gaze was relentless and bright as the blade of a sword.

"But your kisses—your wonderful passion—your insistence—" he stammered.

"It was all for his sake. I tell you, I hated and loathed you."

"It was damned good acting then."

"It could hardly exceed yours during our engagement," she flashed back.

"Acting, no, it was prostitution," he said with a sudden storm of anger, "if what you say now is true."

"Perhaps; you may call it what you please. I would do anything in the world to save a helpless and suffering animal and be proud of it," she answered.

Eric turned away and took a few paces up the long room. She angered him. In a way he longed to strike her for what she said to him, but the memory of last night clung to him and held him. It had been so wonderful, so perfect, her love, real or assumed; she looked now so bright, so true, so undaunted, he longed for her, coveted her more than ever he had done in the past. He could not imagine how they had drifted into this mess. He had tried hard to please her during their engagement and had succeeded. He had won her. How had he lost her so soon? He did not know what to say, nor how to act. And all about this stupid dog; he would kill the beast if he could get hold of it.

"What can we do now?" he said, at last in a tone of bewildered perplexity.

"We must get a divorce. I believe it can be managed somehow. Your wife has eloped, deserted you, refuses to come back, go to a lawyer and see what he can do for you. If those charges are not enough, I have done more for I married a good man, and my wedding night was passed with somebody else, another totally different man. If a lawyer can't twist that into cause for divorce, he can't be much of a lawyer. I don't want to spoil your whole life, so I give you leave to say anything you like about me."

And before he had realised it, she had opened the door and had gone, and though he stormed and swore and summoned the servants and Linda came down to him, nothing would induce Eva to see him again.

She vanished from him and all he could do was to follow her advice and seek consolation of his lawyers.

About a year later, had anyone passed through the scarlet land of poppies at Cromer, he would have seen two girls sitting among them, looking out to the hazy sea, and a great wolfhound lying between them. He has been christened Joy, and his sparkling eye and glossy coat, his rounded form and waving brush of a tail all speak to the appropriateness of his name.

He and Eva are inseparable and he understands her looks, her tones, her words. He understands *her* far better than Eric ever had, and at any moment he would lay down his life joyfully for her sake.

"I see that Eric has married again, Eva," Linda said presently. "So now you are really and truly free. Do you think you will ever marry again, yourself?"

"Not while Joy lives," Eva answered, her little hand resting on his neck and buried in its thick, glossy black hair. "I would never give him a rival. The next man might want to chain him up in the yard! Then we'd have to run away again, wouldn't we, Joy?"

And the great dog leapt to his feet and gave a deep, musical bark in answer, bounding backwards and forwards and leaping up to them as the two girls rose and wended their way slowly through the poppies, emblems of peace and forgetfulness, home.

THE JEWEL CASKET

The wind howled miserably round the great London station and pierced the thin, worn clothing of Jim Thorn and Bill Smith as they loitered, hands in pockets, near the mouth of one of the draughty passages.

It was a bitter January evening and neither inside them nor outside them had the men anything to keep them warm.

"It ain't no sort of use, Bill," remarked Jim, drearily, after a long silence during which both men had been gazing across the wide space filled with moving figures to where the refreshment buffet threw out its warm and cheery glow speaking of the tempting delights within. "We shan't get a job here to-night. There's too many reg'lar porters about." He was a thin, spare man, with a long white face in which shone two grey eyes of a kindly expression. Once a good gardener, ill-health and ill-luck had brought him to evil days.

"Go on with yer! Who came here after a job?" snarled the other, in every way a contrast to his companion: thick-set and heavy, bull-necked, long-lipped and cruel-eyed. "It's pinching we're after and I'll get something to-night or I'm not Bill Smith." Lie finished his sentence with an oath. The other made no reply, only sank into a still more slouching position against the wall. The crowd of passengers before them had swelled. There were many coming out from the ticket office following well-filled trucks of luggage. It was not long now to the departure of a favorite express into Kent. Jim Thorn's gaze drifted about the throng until it lighted on a girl's figure, one of a newly-arrived party, and there it remained. His eyes followed her about with interest, not because he thought she had anything to "pinch," but because, in his own instinctive, uneducated way, he loved all pretty things. She was a very pretty young lady in her plain dark clothes and her heavy furs, with a slim tall figure and golden curly hair peeping out from underneath her small black velvet hat. Jim looked at her with pleasure. He quite forgot about the hot coffee he had been dreaming of in watching her dainty movements.

It did not occur to him to envy her furs or her warm clothing, nor to be wrathful with her that she had them, and he had not. His mind was not of the Socialist order. He no more expected her to give him her cloak than he expected himself to give his coat to one who had only waistcoat and trousers. Her cloak was hers and his coat was his, and could he have explained his mental attitude in words, he would have told you that he was jolly glad that the same law and order that enabled the lady to keep her cloak, also gave him the right to keep his coat and not have it torn off his back by one poorer than he. Although the companion of a thief, he was by nature a respecter of property.

Suddenly he felt a great grab on his arm, and Bill bent his large red face close to him.

"Look there!" he whispered excitedly. "The very thing I was looking for. See that party?"

50

Jim, following with his gaze Bill's outstretched finger, saw to his dismay that it indicated the very young girl he had been so admiring.

"See that little case she has?" pursued his companion in his thick, beery accents. "Mark my words, that a jool case!" His mouth was close to Jim's ear now. "P'raps dimonds, maybe pearls." He let fly these imposing words like darts into Jim's ear.

Jim straightened up and strained his eyes to see what the girl was carrying. It certainly did look most inviting. A little square, rather deep case of some dark wood, clamped carefully on all sides with metal, and with a handle on the top through which the dainty hand of its owner was passed. It looked as if pearls or diamonds might be lying on cotton wool inside, and yet the sentimental Jim felt he did not want that young lady robbed.

"It's a bit small," he ventured lamely, in a discouraging tone.

The burly one gave a contemptuous grunt. "Much good *you'd* be at the game without me," he answered. "Haven't you never heard wot's good comes in small parcels? Don't you know that small and valuable, easy to sell and light to carry should be the pinchers' motto? I'm onto that there jool casket, if I dies for it."

"But you don't know what's in it," argued Jim. "Maybe it's just a purse with not much in, an' a ticket, an' a hanky."

The other sniffed scornfully, his gaze glued on the girl's hand as he answered:

"You just watch, as I do, an' don't talk so much. I've watched and watched that girl till I knows wot's in that casket as well as I knows wot's in my pocket. 'Ow do I know? Well, because she's that careful of it. She looks down at that little box every half-minute and just now, when she set it down for a second and the porter comes by, up she snatches it again and holds it to her, and w'en just now someone wanted to take it off her while she fastened her jacket, she shakes her head and clings on all the time."

"It'll take some doing to get it," replied Jim, with intensifying gloom.

"I can manage it," returned Bill, swelling out his chest. "You'll see. I'll always take trouble for jools, and jools they is. Girls don't go on like that about anything else."

"P'raps it's her young man's picture," suggested the sentimental Jim in a last hope of changing his companion's intention, though the little square box with its clamp did not suggest a portrait-case.

The light from where the men stood was not very good and the dark case sank indistinguishably into the shadow of the girl's dress. Bill could not see to his satisfaction what shape and look it really had but the girl's intense solicitude for it carried complete conviction to his mind which was unable to imagine anything being of value except what could be turned into cash.

The conversation came to an end as the crowd of passengers moved toward the barrier. It was time for action and the two thieves mingled with the stream of hurrying humanity and pressed closely up behind the party to which the girl with the jewel-case belonged. She was certainly very careful of it. She held it tightly and firmly to her so that it could not be caught or brushed out of her grasp by any jostling or hustling movement and she constantly glanced down on it as if to assure herself of its safety. The train had not come up and the throng swayed back again,

Bill and Jim moving naturally with it, but always quite close to the girl. They were, though thinly and poorly dressed, not ragged, or in their aspect in any way likely to attract attention. Bill, especially, had adapted for the occasion quite a traveling appearance and had a light overcoat on one arm. True it was only a bit of an overcoat, but when skilfully draped on the arm, looked quite well and might have its uses. Their quarry now approached the book-stall to the delight of Bill, but though the girl stopped to look with interest at the books and papers and even purchased one of the latter, she never once set down the little box. The train was now due and the passengers thickly bunched near the barrier to the platform. Once through the barrier the girl would be, as Jim put it to himself, "safe," for he really did not want to see that box filched from her slender hand, and as Bill put it to himself, "lorst." He felt desperate and was just inwardly cursing his luck when luck itself favoured him. The girl was standing chatting to the older persons of her group, presumably her parents, when a young man, leading a fat terrier, hurriedly joined the throng round the gates. Bill's eye fell on the dog, and he instantly moved to the side of the girl farthest from the young man. With a movement of his hand he attracted the dog's attention, and next moment the chain was wound round the girl's ankles. The dog-owner pulled at the chain, but to free herself she had to take it from his hand, and to do so, for one moment, she set the box down beside her. In the second, while she stooped over the dog, Bill's great hand dropped on the box. It was lifted and under his hanging coat, and he and Jim sifted themselves out of the press of passengers now swaying to the gates which had just been opened. Calmly, quietly, with blank faces, Jim and Bill crossed the station to the exit, hearing in their rear a sort of confused clamour which told them the owner of the box had discovered her loss.

No one stopped them, no one looked at them. They slipped through the windswept passage, and in a few seconds were out in the street; still without apparent haste, but at a good pace, they turned down a side alley and made a short cut for "home." As they turned down one silent, dark street, Bill, swelling with satisfaction, opened out on his companion.

"Now you see wot it is. But for me you'd never have got this necklace, or tiary, whichever it is, an' we might have stayed grubbin' at 'ome all winter. Now we'll have a trip abroad for it won't do to try and sell 'em here. It ain't safe for pearls and dimonds."

"We don't know yet that they is pearls and dimonds," objected Jim.

"There you go. You haven't the brain to imagine anything," returned Bill loftily. "And what do you think a young lady would be carrying—herself—personally, mind, when she had a strappin' maid walking behind her with a dressing-case a yard square. Maybe you'd have gone for that dressing-case," he added, with a crushing sneer. "That's the ordinary brain all over. Sees what's just ahead an' no more; goes for the gilt-topped bottles and lets the tiarys go. Now p'raps when we've sold the jools and are getting a fling on the Continnong you'll be grateful you've got such a partner and you won't be so narsty about it."

It was a bitter night; sleeting now and with scurries of icy wind and snow. In the sky a moon was struggling up amongst thick black clouds, the streets and alleys through which they passed were slippery, wet and dark. Arrived at a dingy building with a gaping open doorway, they groped their way up an unlighted stone staircase and reached their "pitch" at the top in safety. Bill marched in first with the air of a conqueror, and Jim followed, bolting the door after him. There was a little light from the remains of a smouldering fire in the grate.

Jim stirred it into a blaze and fed it with some split-up egg-boxes, and Bill turned on the gas and lighted it.

"That's my job," he said, setting down the little dark case on the table, "and a neat bit of work I calls it, and that dawg helped wonderful."

Jim regarded it mournfully. Odd though it may seem this strange waif of humanity was not thinking of the rich contents; he was wondering what the poor young lady was feeling at having lost it.

The light revealed a curious den in which these two lived. A folding bed of ancient date with one side sagging to the floor, in the corner. A capacious cupboard in the wall through the half-open door of which strange and various articles were protruding, a table in the centre with scattered tin cups and plates and battered tin teapot on it and on the window ledge a cracked flower-pot with a primrose-root growing in it—Jim's.

"Now, then," said Bill, "let's have a look." He took up the box and turned it round. "Why, blimey, it hasn't a lock," he exclaimed, rather blankly. "That don't look like jools—only a bit of a catch like this, and two 'oles each side. Wot the 'Ell's that for?"

With fingers beginning to tremble, he forced up the brass catch and then tore open the lid, and then both men who had been bending forward over their treasure, collapsed suddenly speechless, on the two chairs, and sat opposite to each other staring across the table, for there within the box was no necklace of rare pearls reposing on velvet cushions, but a neat little nest of hay, from the centre of which looked out with enquiring eyes—two white mice!

Very dainty silk-like coats of the purest white on which the gas-light gleamed, tiny pink paws of the palest shell-like pink, little white ears delicate as a butterfly's wing and large eyes like glowing rubies. Gentle and not dreaming that anyone could hurt them, they looked up at the staring faces of the men over them, unafraid, and began polishing their noses with their tiny paws.

Bill recovered from the shock first. With a foul oath, he sprang to his feet and made a grab at the box, but Jim was too quick for him. With one of his agile movements that made him such an invaluable thief, he snatched away the box before Bill's heavy hand reached it, snapped down its lid and held it firmly in both hands against his chest.

"Wot yer goin' to do with it?" he asked.

For a full ten seconds, Bill swore all the best oaths he knew.

"Do with it?" he roared at the finish. "Throw it on the fire and see those vermin burn alive—you just give it me!"

Jim turned pale and clutched the box tighter.

"Now, Bill, you'd never do such a thing," he urged anxiously. "They's done you no harm and it's crool to burn them; no good'd come of it, besides the lidy was fond of 'em, you saw that yourself, and maybe there'll be a reward. Here's a name and address on the box."

This was sound sense, but Bill was blind and deaf with fury. No oaths nor mere words could suffice to vent his rage. Some horrible violence and cruelty alone could do that. He made a lunge across the rickety table, but Jim avoided him and backed against the wall. He was pale, but his eyes shone with an indomitable light. A frail, small man with a poor physique and little health or strength but there was a spirit in him that had often stood up to and conquered the big bully before. He saw now this might be a fight to the death, but he just felt he didn't care. He would be crushed to a pulp first before Bill got hold of the box and burned those two little innocent things inside. His blood was up and on its tide had risen that wonderful determination that can make one weak man equal to ten strong ones. Bill was round the table in an instant and let fly at him a blow from his ponderous fist which he meant to stretch him senseless, but Jim dodged and it only caught the corner of his eye and his lean arm seemed locked like steel across the box on his chest and Bill wrenched at it in vain.

Does some great current of electricity come into being with that mental fixity of purpose and lend a determined combatant a strength altogether beyond his own?

It seemed so to Jim. He seemed full of some living force as he dodged round the table and chairs and over the bed and Bill came floundering after him, cursing and sending his blows wide of the mark. At last Jim found himself close to the door and with a monkey's quickness shot back the bolt and fell through the opening door. Bill grabbed him by the neck, but Jim wriggled so furiously that both men fell in a heap on the top stair and then rolled to the bottom. As they bumped onto the last step, Bill's hands sank from the other's neck and while Jim scrambled to his feet he lay inert and crumpled on the lowest stair.

Jim, breathless, his thin clothing torn and one eye closed, but still gripping the box to his body, ran out into the street and to the nearest lamp-post. There under the wavering light he read the address on the casket-lid:

MISS TORRINGTON
Hailstone Hall
Sevenoaks, Kent.

All the time Bill had been chasing him round the attic a resolution had been forming in his mind. If he escaped with his life he would take the box and its little inmates back to the young "lidy."

For years past in his low degraded existence this man's soul had vaguely yearned after goodness, as a plant in a dark cellar strains with its colourless leaves towards its native light, but there was little opportunity in his life overshadowed by Bill for anything but crime. He hated Bill but he couldn't get away from him. He had not the strength of mind to say good-bye to the daring pal who kept the attic supplied with bread and beer and knew exactly how to utilise in his petty thievings the sharp agility of Jim. But now to-night was the end of it all. Bill was down and out and the way lay clear to a good action, and standing there in the biting cold with his bleeding eye and bruised body, he thrilled through and through with joy. He had done something already. He had foiled his companion's brutal intention, he had saved the animals, and now if he could restore the "lidy's" property to her safe and sound he felt he would be content no matter what happened to himself. Possibly the thought of a reward struggled for life at the back of his mind, but it was not the prompting motive, and there was a risk of being turned over to the law and to prison on returning the property, which far out-balanced the possible reward. To have kept on the right side of his partner and destroyed the stolen goods, as a business proposition, was far better, but the thought of the lady's pleasure and the joy of the little creatures that had looked out so confidingly at him, attracted him just as the primrose blossoms pleased his eyes when they bloomed in the Spring on his window ledge.

Sevenoaks! Not so far away—a matter of twenty-four mile. He had tramped it before in the hop-picking season; he could tramp it again. It was a freezing night, but the moon was getting up, and if he had luck he would be there in the morning. He raised the lid of the casket and looked in to see if his treasures were still safe. Yes, there they lay close side by side, like tiny snowballs tucked down in the hay which had protected them through all the scuffling with Bill and the roll down the stairs.

Jim carefully snapped to the lid and put the box under his arm for shelter against the searching wind. Then aching and shaky in body but dauntless in mind he set out for his tramp to Sevenoaks. When the city and its pitiless streets were left behind him and he had once reached the open country road he felt happier. Here there were no police to pass with a quaking heart as they sternly eyed his blood-stained face and torn coat. He stepped out more strongly as the night wind of the countryside blew in his face. It was cold but not so damp and cruel as London's breath. He looked over the hedge-tops across the wide meadows with the shadowy form of sleeping cattle; he looked at the trees arching over him and the tracery of their shadows on his path, at the sky with the moon riding high in it through bands of scurrying clouds, and he felt he loved it all. Wonderful indeed, as the Latin poet sang, is the joy of the mind conscious of its own right doing, and wonderful also is the dominion of man's mind over his body. Jim, the poor, penniless tramp, hungry and empty and aching, footsore, weary and cold, marched on full of the greatest joy of his life because his mind told him he was doing right. Many doubts and fears beset him and much anxious questioning as to his reception and his fate but nothing could quell that springing sense of joy in his heart as mile after mile fell behind him. When the first red light of morning lit up the sky, it shewed a forlorn and limping figure with a drawn and haggard face, but with a proud, glad light in its one uninjured eye.

The great gates of Hailstone Hall looked imposing enough, shut tight in frosty splendour of twisted ironwork, but they were not locked and Jim pushed them open with an unfaltering hand. The drive winding between the velvet green of tall evergreen trees and with gleaming bands of sparkling frost on each side, lay before him silent and solitary save for the birds hopping across it, and Jim walked straight up the middle of it and found himself with a beating heart on the steps before the big front door. No slinking round by the back door for him with that proud consciousness of right in his breast. He wanted no delays and parleys with impeding and inquisitive servants. He felt weak and his strength failing; with the last bit of it he wanted to put the box himself straight into the lady's hand, and then what became of him did not seem to matter at all.

The door opened in response to his modest ring and a young footman looked out at him with blank astonishment.

"Please can I see Miss Torrington," said Jim. "I've something for her which she wants very particular."

He had thought this sentence out with care, and it certainly showed ingenuity in its suggestion of the lady's desire to see him.

The door was not slammed in his face as he feared it might be. The young footman held it, still staring at him in silence. As he said afterwards in the servants' hall, "I was that surprised at his cheek coming to the front door in his condition I couldn't say nothing."

At that moment the butler chanced to cross the hall and seeing the open door and the intruder on the steps, approached. A tall, portly man the butler, who would have made about four of Jim. As he came up the frail one clutched still harder the box against his bony ribs. "Good Lord, if she should drop upon me, I'm done," was the thought that dashed through his brain. Nothing of the kind happened, however.

"My good man," said the butler benevolently, "what is it you want?"

Jim repeated his fine phrase, but stammering a little as his weakness gained on him.

"Very good," replied the butler blandly, "Give me what you have and I will give it to Miss Torrington."

Jim's heart thumped, and the hall seemed moving round him, but he stuck to his purpose.

"Twenty-four miles," he stammered with blue lips. "Give it 'er myself."

The butler looked him over. He was a man of some brains, or perhaps he would not have been butler to Miss Torrington on a comfortable salary. He met the clear determined gaze of Jim's one unclosed eye and read perhaps something in it that made him sign to Jim to enter and the footman to close the door. Then he said: "If you wait here I will enquire if Miss Torrington wishes to see you."

Jim stood still as a post just inside the door and erect, though everything was getting uncertain round him, and the footman lounged watching him.

Though a thief by profession and accustomed to be so styled and considered, a feeling of amusement stirred in Jim that the man should mount guard over him here.

"As if I'd steal a thing off 'er," passed through him, and somehow this new feeling of pride and self-respect he had been indulging in was so delightful he thought he would never steal another thing as long as he lived.

Jim did not know how long he waited, but it seemed a world of time, and then a swift, light step came down the stairs and the young lady herself came across the hall towards him. There she was, slim, dark-clothed form and golden hair and slender hand.

"Oh, you've found my box!" she exclaimed in a sweet, soft voice. "Oh, good man! Are they alive and all right?"

Jim stood speechless; the last of his powers seemed deserting him. His voice died in his throat. With both trembling hands he pushed out the precious casket into her eager grasp.

Then all went dark and he fell in a crumpled heap on the whiteness of the marble flooring.

*   *   *   *   *

Bill is now in quod doing seven years for a burglary with violence, but Jim is third gardener at Hailstone Hall, has a sunny room all to himself, and a whole row of primroses on his window sill.

THE VENGEANCE OF PASHT

In the torrid heat of the Egyptian afternoon the desert lay outstretched, a silent, shimmering golden sea. Little wavelets of sand rose from its surface at intervals, curled over and blew away as the scorching desert wind passed by. Otherwise nothing moved nor stirred till the form of a camel outlined itself against the blue sky, walking easily and swiftly and bearing on its back the slight white clothed figure of a girl. She was young and extremely fair, the mass of curls pressed up against the shady hat-brim was gold as the sunshine, the eyes were bright sparkling blue like the sky above, the skin all softness and bloom. She was humming to herself as she rode—she felt so happy, so delightfully alone and free. She had slipped away from the noisy clamoring crowd of tourists with whom she travelled on her little Cook's ticket which had cost her £25 and brought her to this ancient land of old and sacred gods.

She had escaped from the hateful attentions of one of the men of the party and now with a map and a guide book she had started out on the great adventure of finding for herself the obscure and lonely little temple of the Goddess Pasht.

From her childhood she had studied Egyptian history and she knew all about the great Goddess; divine protector of all the feline tribe. Her father had been an Egyptologist of some note and books and pictures of Egypt had been her playthings from her earliest years but what were books and pictures to the delights of being here at last and seeing for herself the rich and glorious temples that have been the wonders of the world for centuries?

She rode on leisurely, accommodating her supple body to the long swinging stride of the camel and the sun slanted slowly to the Western sky behind her. She was thinking how delightful life would be if there were more of this loneliness in it; that horde of chattering companions she was with usually day and night, how she hated it and that one man who pursued her so relentlessly. That wretched man, how she hated him. He was positively spoiling the whole of her tour. Wherever she went she always found that he was there. She never seemed able to escape him. If their little boat had to cross the Nile to reach Thebes, he always managed to secure the seat next to hers. If the party were making an excursion on donkeys, he always rode his up beside hers and once, through pushing up close beside her on a steep bank, he had forced her donkey so near the edge that it had almost rolled over it. It had been so from the very first, this constant pursuit of her and she could honestly feel she had given him no encouragement. His personal appearance on the first day she saw him among the crowd of jolly-faced tourists had repelled her. The long lanky dark hair which was always falling over his pallid forehead, the sinister dark eyes, the peculiarly evil mouth and above all the large lean sinewy hands had filled her with a sense of horror and repulsion.

Even before she had heard what he was, a medical student, and been shocked by his callous conversation, his horrid talk of his cruel experiments on cats. Cats! animals that she particularly loved for their soft, sinuous movements, their beautiful eyes and their deep silent affections.

She shuddered as she thought of him and glanced involuntarily behind her. But here out in the desert there seemed no menace. Only limpid golden light on golden sand met her eye, infinite silence and peace was all around.

She consulted the map; she should be nearing her destination now and after a few more minutes she descried ahead of her the rising mound of sand that marked the site of the half buried temple of Pasht. Rather plain in its architecture and not imposing in size, it is often passed over by the tourist and the sight-seer as unworthy of particular notice, and the long camel ride one has to take to find. But now with its smooth straight walls glowing gold in the magic lights and its dark portal suggesting mysteries within, its lonely situation out here away from any other tomb or temple away from every sign of life, half buried beneath the drifting tide of sand it seemed to the girl most appealing, far more interesting visited thus in its grandeur of desolation than the larger ones she had seen thronged with loquacious dragomen and gaping visitors.

She pulled up the camel and looked around. Everywhere about her amber glory of soundless space.

"Khush" she said gently to the camel and the great docile beast went down on his knees and let her dismount.

She had to descend three steps and then through the great granite doorway she entered the temple.

There were three small horizontal windows, rectangular slits, at the top of the walls near the stone roof on which the sand had piled and the whole of the interior was full of a soft grey light. In the very centre of the small square chamber was the great statue of the Goddess about three times the girl's own size. A seated majestic figure in grey stone, the body that of a woman, bare breasted and with hands resting on its knees, the head and face that of an enormous cat with calm fixed eyes looking out towards the desert beyond the open door. So had it sat gazing in unmoved calm while the centuries rolled by and generations of men turned into dust which the desert wind swept by the temple door.

Pasht sat there silent and alone in her neglected temple. Her worshippers had passed away, the flowers and lights and wreaths of former days were hers no more, the girls who had danced in her honour and flung chains of roses round her feet, where were they now with their dusky slender limbs and dark laughing eyes? Perished and gone but she in her carven stone sat there still, serene and secure.

The girl on first entering could see nothing but after a few minutes when her eyes, accustomed to the soft gloom, took indistinctly the huge form of the great woman-cat towering over her, a sense of awe enfolded her and she dropped into a sitting position near its feet, and gazed up reverently into the curious feline countenance, carved so long ago by some skilled and loving hand.

"Goddess, I love you," she said in a whispering tone after a minute's silent musing, "just as much as any of your old, old long ago worshippers did, and I love all cats all your incarnations. They are the dearest darlings in the world and so misunderstood. Just because they have not the exuberant spirits of the dog, man thinks they can't feel. But deep down in their dark reserved passionate natures, they feel intensely and they love. Oh, how they can love when one understands them! I am glad they were held sacred and worshipped in Egypt! Perhaps I was one of your temple girls, Goddess, in those old, far off times!"

She sat still on the sand, her hands loosely clasped round her knees. She felt so happy to have discovered the temple—and the statue that her father had told her of and all by herself, and happy to be able to sit still and think for which there was generally so little time in this tour with the band of people always being hurried along from one place to another.

This was an interval of calm and rest and she was thoroughly enjoying it. She felt no fear, no sense of loneliness, under the kind grave eyes of the stone deity. She felt protected and with some august companion.

Suddenly in the soft and profound stillness a sound struck upon her and thinking the camel had become restless, she rose and turned to the door. Then drew back with a half uttered exclamation and stood close against the colossal knees of the goddess with horror stamped on her face. In the doorway stood the slim erect figure of a young man in a light grey suit. Not apparently a very horrifying sight but a chill hatred ran all along the girl's veins as she looked at him and her hand grew cold as the stone on which it rested.

He advanced smiling. "This is a treat darling to find you here all alone," he said gaily coming up to her. "What's this old thing here? Why I do believe its a beastly cat," and he stared up impudently into the stately countenance above them.

"Oh, hush! please, it's a statue of the Goddess Pasht."

The young man looked back at her laughing, "Pasht, well who's she and why's she got a cat's head?"

"She was the patron Goddess of cats," said the girl.

"Oh, was she? Well, she won't like me then, I've cut up lots of her protégés, starved them and drowned them and doubled them up with tetanus."

"Please don't tell me about it. I don't want to hear." The girl's lips were white; all her happy smiles and colour had fled.

"Oh they were only ordinary wretched little street cats anyway," rejoined the man lightly.

"How did you come here?" asked the girl. Her eyes were fixed on the stone face above them. Was it only her fancy, or that the light was failing? It seemed to her the countenance had darkened as if with wrath and the calm gaze grown fierce and grim.

"On a camel; same as you did. Oh, you didn't think I was going over to Thebes did you with the rest of the flock, if you weren't there? Not much. I just waited about in the Hotel and after you'd gone I found out from the porter whom you'd hired the camel from, then I went to *him* and found out where you had headed for. Then I followed you but I had to be precious careful you didn't turn round and see me. One can see for such miles in the desert."

"Why did you come?" the girl's voice was strained and low. Oh, how she hated this man who had made her life a burden ever since the beginning of the tour.

The man laughed.

"What a question! As if you don't know, you little humbug! Why to make love to you of course, not to see this old Smash Pash or whatever you said her name was."

"Well you know I don't want to listen to you and its getting late now. Let us ride back." She was still standing by the knees of the statue. He was between her and the door, she could not move towards it without approaching him.

She glanced round; the greyness of the temple was of a darker tint; outside the glowing patch of light showed the approach of sunset.

"Not at all. I have no intention of going back yet. You may as well sit down and be sensible. I've come out to ask you again will you marry me?"

"No, I have told you before I will not."

"Why?"

"Because I don't love you. I could never love anybody who cut up animals alive."

"We don't call it that now, you are so old fashioned, we call it Scientific Research."

"It's the same thing whatever you call it."

"Lots of women admire it."

"Well marry one of them."

"I don't want to, I want to marry you."

"You can never do that."

"We shall see. To-morrow morning you will be begging and praying me to marry you."

The girl went deadly cold all over and the sweat broke out on her forehead. He had come a little nearer. Through the dark she could see the evil face, the horribly eager expression.

"What do you mean?" she stammered, her throat was dry, her limbs trembled. Horror and hatred and a nameless fear possessed her. The temple seemed growing smaller, its walls contracting, pushing him upon her.

"I should think you'd know. We're going to make a night of it here and if you're alive in the morning—well, we'll see what you say then."

There was a great dead silence. Now that she realized the extremity of her danger her courage seemed to rise to meet it. She thought rapidly: Was there any escape, any help anywhere? Was anyone likely to come to her rescue? Would she be missed, followed?

"You arranged it all very well," the man's voice went on in mocking tones as if in answer to her thoughts. "You told no one where you were going. Only the camel man has the least idea where you are and I've tipped him well. He won't tell anyone *in time*."

He was very near her now and suddenly he threw both arms round her and drawing her up to him kissed her violently on the mouth. At the touch of his lips a perfect fury of revolt rose in her and she struck out wildly at him with her clenched fists. With the strength that the madness of anger gives she wrenched herself loose from him and fled behind the statue so that the colossal form of the image was between her and her tormentor. There she paused trembling and gasping.

The man was now by the knees of the statue. She saw his dark face and the black brows contracted into a straight savage line as the light from one of the slit-like windows above fell on it. He followed her but terror lent wings to her feet and she fled away before he could reach her circling round the image. He followed and dodged and circled also but she was too quick and fleet in her movements for him to circumvent. So for a few moments they played in a deadly game round the age old Deity. But the girl felt her strength failing. The poisons of hatred and anger, terror and loathing were pouring into her blood, enervating her, taking away her powers. Her eyes were darkening, her limbs giving way.

In another moment she must faint and fall.

They were on opposite sides now. Across the lap of the Goddess she saw the crimson face, the bulging blood-shot eyes of the human beast waiting to spring on her. The temple was going dark, all was whirling before her.

"Save me, Pasht!"

And as her agonized scream rang through the temple, she pressed her slender white hands against the arms of the statue.

Was it the pressure of those soft fingers disturbing the balance already shaken by the shifting of the sand floor through a thousand years? Or was the stone heart of the Goddess turned to flesh and blood as man's heart is so often turned to stone? Who shall say?

Before the murderous beast could move back from where he stood beside her lap the huge idol reeled and fell over on its side with a sullen thud bearing him to the ground beneath its six tons of solid granite. The temple shook to its foundation and the whole air was filled with a fog of blood and sand. One piercing shriek of agony rang through it. Then there was silence except for the sound of the blood thrown on the walls trickling down them to the ground. The concussion of the air in that small space had thrown the already half fainting girl back against the wall. For a moment she could see nothing, the stinging sand filling and closing her eyes. Then as the particles settled down once more to their age old repose her terrified gaze took in the form of the huge image at her feet, the scarlet wall opposite her, the semi-obliterated mass of small human form and clothes. The man's face was crushed deeply into the sand under the colossal shoulder of the Goddess but something still moved, chaining her fascinated gaze —two large sinewy hands scrabbled still convulsively pulling at the sand. Then after a few more minutes these also grew motionless. Breathless, terrified, half suffocated and dazed the girl still clung to the wall hardly realising yet what had happened and if she herself were still living and uninjured. Then as the sand settled and the air grew clear, calmness returned to her and she knew she was safe and free.

With gentle steps she approached the huge fallen form, avoiding the horrid blue hands that looked still able to grip and grasp and holding her skirts away from all the contamination oozing from under the stone and looked down into the face of the statue. The light from the doorway slanted on to it and seemed to soften it all into smiles and the desert wind springing up passed through the temple and out at the top slits by the roof with a loud purring sound. The girl stooped and pressed her warm red lips on the ancient stone brow in a kiss of gratitude, then passed out into the sunset and mounting her camel and followed by the other, rode away over the golden sand and night settled slowly on the desert in a violet dusk enclosing the ancient temple where the Goddess Pasht lay purring on her prey. Her starry eyed children were avenged.

VILLAGE PASSION

The shapely mass of her body was outlined dark against the rosy gold of the evening sky, as she sat on the top of the red brick orchard wall, looking up and down the country road on which it bordered.

She was named Apricot Marten and the Christian name given her by a fanciful mother could not have been more suitably bestowed. She was just like a golden glowing apricot in its very best condition when it hangs basking in the summer sun. She had a soft, clear skin with a warm flush in the velvet cheek, great lustrous laughing eyes of a warm golden brown, and a wealth of bright waving hair in which the sunrays seemed to have got permanently entangled. Her mouth was bright crimson and turned up at its smiling corners, and her body was supple and gracious in its full rounded contours. Altogether she was an enchanting piece of girlhood just merging into womanhood, and many were the sleepless nights passed by the young men of Fullingham village in thinking about her.

She was not entirely free from the reputation of a flirt, but deep in her heart her choice was made, and from it she never swerved however mischievously she might behave.

It was John Macpherson the Highlander, the lithe, agile, black-haired, hasty-tempered Scot who worked on the farm which adjoined her father's cottage and orchard. But she gave this away to no one, and many thought she had her eye on Tony Morrison, whose father owned the little village shop and general store, and, in absence of all competition, did a good business. Tony served in the store, and while rather short and insignificant in physique, made up for this by the extreme care he bestowed upon his dress and personal appearance. He wore neat and becoming grey suits and townish-looking hats, and always produced a pleasing impression of great cleanliness and smartness. Tony's heart had been given long ago to Bessie Smith in the next village, a little quiet mouse of a girl with violet eyes. Apricot was much too flamboyant a personage to please his quiet taste, but this secret devotion he also imparted to no one, and as Apricot was considered the belle of his village, it flattered his masculine vanity to be supposed one of her accepted admirers. By a quiet and modest smile he generally managed to encourage the rumours about himself and Apricot while ostensibly denying them. All of which made the heart of John Macpherson flare up with consuming anger against him.

Thus stood matters in Fullingham village on that lovely summer evening when Apricot sat humming to herself on the top of the orchard wall. The scene was truly idyllic in its beauty. Fullingham is one of the prettiest villages in the quietest and most remote part of Devonshire, and this evening the glory of pink light in the sky was so great it turned even the white road a rosy colour, and all the hedges were full of wild roses and the still warm air heavy with balmy scents.

Apricot thought it beautiful, and looked with longing eyes up and down the road. She felt she wanted to kiss somebody, to throw her arms round somebody's neck, and who so delightful for this as the handsome Highlander, if he would only come! They had an appointment at this place and hour. She was there, but where was he? There was no one to be seen in the road except a small shock-haired boy gnawing an apple. Then, swinging lightly along, came a figure down the road.

Apricot put her hand to shade her eyes to see, but it was not John. She thought at first it was Tony, that slight, neat form in grey with the smart hat; but no, it was not he. It was a stranger.

Up went Apricot's hand to her hair to smoothe back a tress. What would he think of her? She wondered. Would he look up as he passed?

The stranger did more than that. When he came up to the orchard he stopped and looked up.

"What are you doing up there?" he asked. His voice was gentle and courteous, and the face he turned up towards her very pleasant to look at.

Apricot did not resent his addressing her.

"What's that to you?" she called back saucily, showing her small white teeth in a gay smile; and pulling a great red rose that grew on the wall close to her hand, she threw it down full in his face.

The stranger caught the rose and kissed it, and then stuck it in his coat.

"Come down and have a little walk with me. You look lonely up there."

"Not so lonely as you look in the road, young man."

"Oh, I'm lonely enough! That's why I want your company."

"Will you catch me?" she said laughing and leaning over.

"Certainly I will," he answered, holding out his arms. "Come along."

She swung her shapely legs and neat feet over the side of the wall next him, and then let herself slip down it. He caught her fine, well-developed figure in his arms, and holding her up tight and close gave her a kiss on her bright red lips.

She slapped his face, but quite gently, and struggled away from him, shaking her blue cotton gown straight that had been rather rumpled by her descent.

"Now we'll go for a walk," said the stranger. "Which way?"

"Oh, we'll go towards Hawley village. That's very pretty," she answered. "And if you want the train you can get it there. You're a town gentleman, aren't you?" she added shyly.

Fullingham village is off the railway line and it was not an uncommon thing for strangers to pass through the village from Riverside where there was a station to Hawley on the other side where they could again take the train, having walked through six miles of the prettiest Devonshire scenery.

"Oh, that'll do very well. I didn't know you had a train so near. Yes, I'm finishing my holiday and going back to town to-night."

They were walking slowly up the road now in the gorgeous sunset light. A moon large and pale as a thin white paper disc rose in the East before them.

Apricot had her own ideas in view in going in the Hawley direction and shipping the stranger off her hands there. She was thoroughly enjoying the new sensation of walking and talking with a London gentleman, but she was not *quite* sure how John Macpherson would view her little promenade, and she was not *too* anxious to be met or seen by him. It was quite true he had not kept their tryst, and in her own mind that quite excused her for going off with someone else. But then, he and she did not always agree about these things, and altogether it was best to take the handsome stranger out of her own village and over to Hawley in which direction the Fullingham rustics did not often walk.

Laughing and jesting and walking quite near together the two young figures passed up the sunlit road. Some little way ahead of them there was a fork, one road winding up an incline and passing through a larch plantation on the hill before it dipped down to Hawley station, the other a far prettier road following the valley and passing through a lovely wood as it worked round to Riverside.

Apricot and the stranger walked along with springing steps, taking the Hawley road. It was surely an evening to feel, if ever, the madness of Summer in one's veins. He thought he had never seen such a lovely country girl and she, without swerving in the least from her allegiance to the fiery Macpherson, thought it was the greatest fun in the world to be admired by a town gentleman, a real London man, with London clothes and all.

"There'll be none of this when I'm married to John," she was reflecting inwardly. "Best have what fun I can now."

Heated a little by their walk up hill in the warm Devonshire air, they entered the feathery larch plantation with a feeling of relief. It was full of light, shade and music; thrushes and blackbirds, robins and chaffinches not yet exhausted by their nesting cares were trilling on every side of them.

"Let's sit down here," he suggested as they came to a mossy bank where a tiny brooklet tinkled by, and Apricot, flushed and lovely, sat down willingly and let the stranger's arm come round her waist. Her conscience told her it was not quite right, but oh! that wood with its rosy mystery of softened summer light and the wandering perfumes of roses and hot resin and the magic of the birds' voices, all talking of love, what girl would not be swayed by it and made a little giddy by the sweet intoxication of it all?

Meantime, Macpherson had gone down to the store, his work being over at the farm for that day, to buy himself a new tie wherewith to charm Apricot at the trysting. He was much put out to find there only one tie and that green, a colour he thought didn't suit him. Everyone knows the kind of village shop it was where everything is sold, but things are so seldom what one wants. Gloves are there, but only size ten. Boots are there, but only size four. Pencils are sold out, but you can have a slate pencil. Bootlaces have not come in, but you can have a ball of string. Macpherson bought his tie, and as the gawky girl who assisted Morrison, was wrapping it up in a bit of paper too small for it, he asked:

"Where's Tony?"

"Gorn sweethearting, I 'spects," answered the girl with a grin, "leastways, he went out all dressed up in his new soot and hat."

Macpherson grunted, paid and left, went home, donned the tie, and then, a little late, flustered and rather put out, hurried to the appointed orchard wall. There was no Apricot—no one to be seen at all up or down the wide country road except a small boy devouring the core of an apple. Macpherson waited with glowering eyes. It was all very well for him to be a bit late. He had a man's work to do, but girls should be punctual.

Several minutes went by, each an hour to the waiting man. Then he strode across to the boy on the other side.

"You seen Miss Apricot about here?" he asked.

The boy looked up stolidly. "I seed her a while ago."

"Where?"

"On yon wall," answered the boy, nodding in that direction.

"Well, where did she go?"

"Nowhere, till a gent comed along; then there wur a lot of huggin' and kissin' an' she went off with he."

Macpherson's face was a study as he listened to this astounding statement. He stood rooted to the spot, and from his six feet glowered down on the malicious little imp in the road as if he could kill him. The boy knew perfectly well that Macpherson was "sweet" on Miss Apricot, and he thoroughly enjoyed imparting this information. He would have been afraid to make up such a story, but since he had witnessed it all and it was perfectly true and this great giant had asked him, he was going to have the fun of telling him, on the same principle that he egged on Farmer Smith's dog to fight another dog and shook the bag when he was carrying ferrets to make them attack each other.

He was a little alarmed when Macpherson's great paw came down heavily on his shoulder.

"You little rat! What sort of a man was it? Tell me that!"

"I dunno," said the boy sullenly, trying to shake himself free, "a kind of a smart chap in a grey soot and hat."

"A grey suit and hat!" The light blazed in Macpherson's dark eyes. He shook the boy by the shoulder.

"Was it Tony Morrison at the store?"

"I dunno," wailed the boy frightened now by the awful look of rage in the man's face and only anxious to get away. "I never go to the store, muvver always goes."

Another frightful shake that made his teeth rattle.

"Was it?"

"I dunno. I never saw 'is face, only 'is back as he was a-kissin' of her. It mout be the store man, or it moutn't."

"Little devil!" growled Macpherson, and with a final shake sent the boy down on his hands and knees in the dust. Then he strode off up the road at a tremendous pace, his blood on fire, his mind entirely made up.

It was Tony, of course. He knew that absolutely. He was convinced of it. The grey suit and hat, the smart appearance—who else in Fullingham had that? It was Tony's own particular property and asset. Besides, had he not just heard at the store that Tony was gone sweethearting? Of course it was all quite clear. Huggin' and kissin' his Apricot! The thought of her darling velvet cheek that he himself so reverently touched, her lovely smiling scarlet mouth, came to him and seemed to add boiling oil to the raging flame within him. He would do for him! He would kill him! He would break his back! The cur! The reptile! Who all along had been carrying on with his girl and who was so smug and so satisfied—always at the store so neat and clean, and always so civil-spoken and so quiet!

He had always rather liked Tony. There had been a great friendship between the men only lately a little spoiled by the slumbering suspicion in John's mind that Tony might be "after his girl," but Tony had always been good to him personally and he always spoke of Apricot to John as Miss Marten, which came back bitterly to John now. "I'll 'Miss Marten' him when I catch him," he said between his teeth.

A hideous thing is jealousy, blinding its victim, deafening him alike to the voice of conscience and the voice of reason hounding him on to the scaffold and the grave.

John Macpherson, good man, great soul, walked up the road that evening with red murder in his heart. When he came to the cross-roads he stopped and hesitated. Which way had they gone?

He decided they must have taken the road to Riverside. It lay before him so attractively beautiful all bathed in golden sheen; the road to Hawley was up hill and in shadow.

Before one reaches Riverside comes the wood, and as the road passes into it there is a low stile. On this stile with his back to the road and all unconscious of the desperate figure of vengeance striding along it, sat a figure in grey. It was Tony, blissfully happy; full of light-hearted innocent enjoyment swinging his legs to the tune he was whistling. He was looking back to Riverside and was counting the kisses shy little Bessie had given him that day, and thinking how sweet she had looked when she promised to marry him. Now he was on his way home to Fullingham and just pausing to rest on the stile and enjoy the sweet calm and peace of this perfect evening which suited so well his happy mood.

Suddenly as John came along the road he caught sight of the grey back rising above the stile and every drop of blood in John's body turned to raging flame. His ears caught the gay whistle. Apricot was nowhere to be seen, but that was natural. She would be slinking home through the woods by way of Riverside and back to her father's cottage, where she would turn up with the innocent look of the cat who has stolen the cream. Well, nothing could be better. Apricot out of the way he could deal all the more swiftly and better with his rival.

Like a bull at a fence he rushed at the stile, and Tony was knocked off and down on the ground, pinned under John's hands at his throat before he knew who had approached.

"You weasel! You little devil! I'll kill you!" John stormed, and lifting the prostrate man by the neck dashed him down again with all his force. There was a wide stone flag just under the stile to help matters in the muddy wintertime, and on this flag Tony's head came down with a good bang.

"What's up?" he gasped, as well as he could with John's suffocating grip on his neck. "What's this for, Mac?"

"Huggin' and kissin'!" ground out John between his teeth. "I'll teach you to come after my girl!"

"I haven't! I haven't!" cried Tony. "Let up, Mac, let up! You're mad."

"If I'm mad you're dead. I'm going to kill you, you little beast!" Bang! "Where were you this afternoon?" Bang! "Answer me that." Bang!

Tony's lips were going white. His thoughts were scattered by the blows on his head. He managed to gasp out: "Riverside! I've been to Bessie—I haven't seen your girl."

"You're a good liar," scoffed John. "You were seen huggin' my girl and I'll see you never do again. Now go on with more of your lies." Bang! Bang!

But Tony's lying or speaking at all had come to an end. His face went grey; his jaw dropped; his body fell limp in the fierce hands which held him.

John let him slide down and struggled to his feet. Instantly his rage fell from him. He was face to face with the awful fact—he had killed a man.

Sane now, calm, his anger utterly spent and gone from him, John stood panting there, looking about him. He was quite alone in the golden evening; everything was exquisitely calm about him, a thrush near by was pouring out his song, and the figure, a few moments before sitting whistling on the stile, was now lying limp and motionless at his feet. Those few moments of blind, dark rage had turned one man into a corpse, the other into a murderer.

Murder! It was hanging for that.

A wild longing to undo what he had done possessed him. He went down on his knees.

"Tony!" he called. "What's the matter with you? Tony, wake up!" But the man lay still and grey before him. He undid his coat and felt his heart; there was no movement.

He passed his trembling arm under his head and raised him and put his own face down close to see if any breath touched his cheek; but there was none. Limp, nerveless, the body lay across the flagstone, seeming to ask him, "What will you do with me now?" And John, wrapped in that awful horror, that awful responsibility of his deed, rose from his knees and stood shuddering by the stile.

Then terror came and seized him. He must conceal his act. He must hide the body. It must never be known he had murdered Tony. He might never be discovered. If Tony's body were found later, in the wood, what would tie this deed to him, Macpherson? Tony might have been murdered by a tramp in the wood.

Shivering as if with mortal cold, John stooped over the body and dragged it by the shoulders out of the path, and into the little wood. Parting the flowering bushes by the side of the track, he pushed into the thick undergrowth and there left the motionless form under some wild azaleas.

Then with, the cold, clammy fingers of his crime clinging to him, unnerved and shaken, with his heart in a black terror, he crept out, a criminal, from the shade of the trees and took the sunfilled road again.

He looked all round the stile, but there was no trace of the crime committed there. He brushed the white dust of the path from his own clothes. Then he stood and listened.

Not a sound to mar the lovely serenity of the golden air. Even the thrush had finished his beautiful song and all was silence.

*　　*　　*　　*　　*

John Macpherson, the same in outward appearance, but within a miserable, broken and craven man, entered the village pot-house as the sunset faded and the moon grew brighter, and called for a glass of beer.

When he got it he took it to one of the side benches, where he sat down away from the rest of the company and swallowed it in silence.

What an awful sense of guilt clung round him; but the man deserved it, he kept telling himself. Why did he come sneaking round after another man's girl? If it ever came out that he had killed him, everyone would allow that he had been sorely tried. As he sat there, black and moody, with eyes fixed on the sawdust-covered floor, scraps of conversation floated over to him from the bar where the men had gathered. He heard nothing at first; then a sentence pierced his preoccupied brain.

"Smart young fellow, wasn't he? Did you see him, Bill?"

And then Bill's answer struck dully on his ears:

"I just seed him go by. I was at the window there, an' I looks up. 'Why, there's Tony, ses I' bein' as 'ow he was all togged up in grey. And I calls out, 'Tony!' 'cos I wanted them bootlaces he promised me. And the feller turns round and I couldn't help larfin', for it wasn't Tony at all, but this other chap."

There was a general laugh at Bill's expense.

"I could have told you Tony was off for the day. I met him going to Riverside just after dinner-time."

"An' what was this young feller doin' down here, this London chap, I mean?" came another question.

"Oh, just walking through Fullingham, as they do, you know, to see the country. He went up by Marten's orchard last thing I see of him, going to Hawley, for sure."

The talk drifted on then; but John Macpherson, seated near the open door whence the delicious balmy air, heavy with the scent of new-mown hay, came in and mixed with the beer and baccy of the bar, grew cold with horror as he sat and heard. An icy conviction gripped him to his inner being strangling him.

He had killed the wrong man!

He knew it. He felt sure of it. Tony's gasping words came back to him backed up now so unexpectedly by this man at the bar. Tony had been to Riverside, he had "gorn sweethearting" but to his own legitimate property, his own girl. It was the other man in grey who—oh, the horror of it! He'd go mad if he sat there another minute. He got onto his feet and was just about to cross the threshold when another phrase from the little knot of men arrested him. They had got onto a prize-fight now. They were discussing it, as one of the men had seen it in a neighboring town.

"And there he lay, and nothin' they could do seemed to bring him round. I thought he was dead, sure. Then another bloke comes along, and whether he tips brandy down 'is throat or what he does, I don't know; but up springs my fine fellow as gay as you please, and they sets to again."

A sudden ray of hope seemed to split the darkness in John's mind. Suppose— suppose Tony was not quite dead? Oh! the wonderful joy of the thought. Suppose, like that other man, he could come round! Oh, if such a thing might happen now and let him out of this cold cell of terror he seemed shut up in, he swore within himself he would never lift hand against man, woman or child again!

He had his whiskey-flask in his pocket. Full of a new determination he turned and walked to the bar.

"Six-penn'orth?" asked the barman, as John handed him the flask.

"Fill it right up, man," said John briefly. And when this was done and paid for, he turned and went out without a word.

The barman shook his head. "Macpherson looks bad to-night," he remarked.

"Bin drinkin' perhaps; or p'raps that girl's leading him a dog's life. She's a termagant."

Outside John sped up the road, new hope, dim, faint uncertain, but still hope glimmering in his heart. The full moon was up in a rich purple sky, and the night was soft and full of beauty. But John could see nothing. He felt the hangman's cord about his neck, and for the wrong man—the wrong man!

All seemed quite still, calm as he had left it when he reached the wood. The silvery light filtered gently through the leaves and fell on his little path, showing him the way.

He stepped aside to the clump of azaleas and pushed them back. There lay the still body, just as he had left it. It had not stirred.

With a thumping heart and a prayer on his lips John knelt beside it, and raising the head pushed the neck of the open flask between the pallid lips.

There was no movement, but some seemed to go down the throat, but he could not be sure. Then he got desperate, and getting his handkerchief just soaked it in the spirit and rubbed it violently all over the man's face and eyes.

"Tony man, wake up, I say!" he muttered, scrubbing his forehead with the fiery spirit.

At last, oh, God! that was a sigh! He was breathing!

John's hand trembled so that he nearly spilt the rest of the flask.

Tony opened his eyes.

"Why, what's this?" he uttered faintly. "Where am I?"

"Here, drink some more," said John feverishly, tipping the flask up and sending a fresh stream down Tony's throat.

He never touched spirits and it burnt him like fire.

He sat up, John supporting him, and looked round. "Is that you, Mac?" he said. "Oh, I remember. You nearly bashed me to death under the stile. What's it all about, Mac?" His voice was rather weakly; his eyes wandered over John's anxious face and then up to the tracery of boughs over them.

"It was all a mistake, Tony, and I am more sorry than I can say. But you're not hurt much, are you?"

Tony was sitting up now. His face looked very white. His hat, carefully picked up by Macpherson and put beside him under the azaleas, was there still. His forehead looked damp, and the whiskey-soaked locks of hair hung loose over it. He leaned his cheek on his hand as he answered:

"I'll have you up before the beak for this," he said calmly. Tony was mostly calm.

"You won't?" exclaimed John anxiously.

"It's six months' hard for 'sault and battery, and it's two years quod for manslaughter," remarked Tony.

John felt a cold sweat break out on him.

"But I've said it was a mistake," he urged. "I thought it was you—" Then he began to stammer. After all, Apricot was his girl and he was not going to give her away.

"Well, why didn't you find out before you came and knocked me about?" asked Tony in an aggrieved voice. "Spoiled my hat, too." And he took it out from the azaleas and smoothed its battered brim in his hands.

"Look here, Tony," said John desperately, "you must overlook this. Not a word must come out. Say how I can make up to you and I'll do it."

"There's that fifty pounds you've saved up," remarked Tony mildly, still stroking his hat.

John fell back flabbergasted. Fifty pounds! The savings of his whole life! The sacred sum put by so that when it grew to a hundred he could set up house with Apricot!

"What do you mean?" he asked with trembling lips.

"It won't be nice doin' hard for six months; and it's two years if they bring it in manslaughter."

"But I didn't kill you, man! They can't call it that!"

"You meant to, though; and you nearly did me in. Oh, my head! it do feel bad!" And Tony leant against a bush beside him and closed his eyes.

John seized his flask and made him take another gulp.

"You better take me home," he said weakly. "I'd like to die in the old house."

John was desperate.

"Look here, Tony, if you don't die and don't say a word you shall have the fifty, I promise you."

Tony straightened himself a little.

"I'll do my best, Mac," he said feebly. "How soon can I have the money? Soon as I've got it I'll say I had a fit; then if I dies you're safe, anyway; and I'll leave Bessie the fifty."

"You're a cool one," growled out John. "Fifty pounds is a lot of money, Tony."

"Well, don't pay it, don't pay it, Mac. Maybe you'll find it all right in quod. Two years ain't long, you know."

Cold shivers went down John's spine. Prison for one of the Highland Macphersons! And Apricot alone and unprotected for two years! She'd never wait for him; nor would old Marten ever let him have his daughter then. He knew Tony had some knowledge of the law. His grandfather had been a solicitor in a small way, and on this account many were the knotty points referred to Tony by the villagers. But he hated like anything to lose his cherished fifty, and made another effort.

"Look here," he said, "I don't see what's to prevent my denying the whole thing. It's your word against mine."

Tony shook his head solemnly. "I'd have the truth on my side, and the truth's a fierce thing to be up against."

John considered. He felt that Tony was right. He could never stand up and call God to witness that he had not laid a finger on Tony. He felt he'd be struck dead or blind if he did.

"An' a man's dying oath is always took in evidence," added Tony in a mournful tone.

"How can it be a dyin' oath if you don't die?"

"If I *think* it's my dyin' oath it's the same thing."

"'Spose it all comes out, anyway?"

"Can't," said Tony, sitting up and speaking with more vigour. "I'f I gets your fifty I'm mum unless I feels like dyin'. If it's that way, I'll say I have had a fit; and if I say it's a fit, a fit it is."

John gave in. "All right," he said with a long sigh. "I'll get you the money to-night. Now let's get back."

He assisted Tony to his feet and put his battered hat on his head.

"Oh, it do ache!" groaned Tony.

"That's all the whiskey you've drunk," returned John unsympathetically.

"Maybe it is, and maybe it's the bashing it's had," returned Tony. And after that, in silence, the two men emerged from the wood onto the moonlit road.

John walked along in black gloom, pondering alternately on his lost fifty and on Apricot.

He wondered if she had walked as far as Hawley with the stranger; if she had got back home by now; if there was the smallest chance of his seeing her to-night. He thirsted for the touch of her red lips to console him for all he had suffered in emotion that day.

Oddly enough he did not feel angry with her. It is a curious point of ethics with the lower classes that what is done with a gentleman does not count. There is not considered to be anything serious about it; it's only "a bit of a lark"; and while the thought of Tony supplanting him had filled him with red fury against him, he had nothing at all against the gentleman from town who had stolen a kiss from his girl in passing through the village. In fact, far away in the recesses of his heart there burnt a spark of pride that Apricot's beauty could not be resisted by anyone.

The two men reached the village with hardly a word exchanged, Tony occasionally stopping to lean on his companion's arm.

John left him at the store and went dolefully enough to fetch the price of his folly. He brought over the small tin box in which he had saved it and added to it through so many years, and put it into the other's hands in the back bedroom behind the shop. He could not bear to see it counted out by the smiling Tony, but with a hoarse mutter of: "It's all there. Mind you keep your word, durn you!" he hurried away.

The night was exquisitely lovely, full of sweet scents, and all the whispers of Summer in the air. He walked past Marten's orchard and looked longingly up to the wall where the trees hung their branches heavy with fruit over the top.

But there was no one to be seen, and finally he walked away disconsolately back to the farm.

All the next day he longed to see Apricot; but it was not till the evening when all the village was dipped in soft violet shadows that he at last met her, just as she was coming out of the store. She looked so lovely his heart rose in a great bound, and he threw his arm around her and pressed his lips into the side of her creamy neck.

"What you been to the store for?" he asked jealously.

"Only for a bit of ribbon; but I stopped to talk to Tony. Oh, John! Think! He's going to marry Bessie Smith in a month, and he's got fifty pounds to start house-keeping! Some folks do save wonderful, don't they?"

"Yes, and some has things given 'em," said John savagely. "But we'll be getting married, too. What would you say if I put the banns up to-morrow?"

Apricot lifted two soft arms and put them about his neck. They were sheltered by an old oak that grew near the store, and there was no one to see. Her upturned face and glowing eyes looked very fair and sweet in the dusk.

She loved her John and meant to marry him, and no one else in this world, but walks and talks like yesterday's with the stranger were very great fun and she was afraid they might be few and far when she was Mrs. Macpherson. Her scarlet mouth closed on John's as she murmured back:

"I think I'd say, John dear, don't be so hasty!"

SUPPING WITH THE DEVIL

CHAPTER 1

"Here, Jenkins, take this animal!" And the body of the dog from which one foreleg had been cut away was thrown into the arms of the new laboratory attendant.

The dog was screaming wildly and some of its blood splashed upon Jenkin's white smock frock and some into his no less white face. The great scientist Sir Charles Smith-Brown Bart. Dsc. F.R.C.S. etc., etc., was at work in his laboratory and his new attendant was assisting him.

It was Sunday morning and the Great Man was rather afraid he might be made late for church by the bungling slowness of his subordinate.

"Throw him into the trough, man, don't stand there staring and clamp down his paws so that he can't move, the three he's got left anyway," he added with a little chuckle. Sir Charles was always cheerful and pleasant at his work. Jenkins turned, lowered the dog into the trough on his back and taking each leg fastened it into the iron clamp provided on each side. The dog was screaming in agony and Jenkins' fingers trembled as he did the clamps and turned his head away that he might not see the beseeching terror in the animal's eyes. It did not seem right somehow. He had fed the little spaniel last night and thought what a jolly little beast it was, frisking round him, and caressing him with its soft nose and tongue. This Sunday morning's work did not seem right to him, but then he was a new hand, only having been engaged last night and having had his duties described to him as "the care of animals."

"Now then have you got him fixed?" asked the great man, coming up behind him, with a keen looking knife in his hand. With this he pointed to the dog's head.

"Bind his jaws and clamp the head, that's right. Now my friend—" the great man leant over the trough in which the dog lay rigid, helpless, extended on its back, its legs clamped to the sides of the trough, wide apart. Jenkins turned away and stared stolidly at the piece of bright blue sky that appeared above the frosted panes of the lower part of the window.

The dog unable to scream with its bound jaws could still moan and a groaning moan of direct agony came to Jenkins' ears as the great man bent over the trough.

When he looked round he saw there was a great gash all down the chest and stomach, laying bare the inside, and in the open cavity the scientist was fumbling with both hands.

"There now that'll do for the present," he said cheerily as he withdrew them, covered with blood, and wiped them briskly on a towel, "I shall have to be off to church now or I shall be late."

"And what about the dog, Sir?"

"Oh, I'll leave him like that. I always do. Let 'em cool off a bit you know," again the pleasant laugh. "Then I'll have at him again after lunch."

He was taking off his white smock in which he worked and revealed himself well dressed underneath. He walked to the wash handstand with its fine brass taps and washed his hands carefully. Then he went into the hall outside where his frock-coat and tall hat were hanging. Jenkins followed him eyeing him uneasily.

"Of course, Sir," he began rather hesitatingly, "I'm new to this kind of work and p'raps I don't understand it, but isn't it a bit cruel?"

The great man had slipped on his fine well made coat over his large comfortable self and was just settling above his eyebrows his very polished new silk hat. He looked back pleasantly at the nervous, puckered face of his subordinate.

"My dear Jenkins you decidedly are new to it, very: but I trust you will improve in time." He took off his pince-nez and held them lightly in one hand, as he was wont to do when addressing a class. "But I don't like these signs of squeamishness. Now I'll just ask you a few questions. You don't know anything about Scientific Research do you?"

"No, Sir," returned Jenkins humbly.

"Well, then," pursued his employer genially, "you must remember Scientific Research is a very noble work and that's what I am doing here, a very noble work," he repeated, "read the daily papers, they are always saying so." Here he waved his pince-nez airily and smiled.

Jenkins was not an adept at analysing sarcasm but as he looked at the smiling doctor and heard his pleasant tones, he had a vague idea that the big man was "making game of him."

"Then another thing is its all for the benefit of humanity. Now remember that, Jenkins, because it's a useful phrase, the benefit of humanity. I am working for the benefit of humanity. You must get that well in your head. All you saw this morning, all you will see here while you are with me is all for the benefit of humanity, see?"

Jenkins feeling himself confused and baffled by the smiling eyes and suave tones, tried to keep hold of his point.

"Still it is cruel, isn't it, Sir?" he mumbled.

"Cruel?" repeated the Doctor with a shade of impatience. "Certainly *not*. Supposing it were cruel what an uproar there would be! You know what a lot of churches there are, all full of God-fearing clergymen, good holy men. Would they allow it if it were cruel? Of course not. They would denounce it in their sermons but they never say a word against it. They uphold it. To-day for instance all the London churches are full of these good men talking themselves hoarse, telling us all what we must not do, but you won't find one saying we must not pursue our researches."

"P'raps they don't know what you are a doin' of," blurted out Jenkins and then paused alarmed at what his employer would think of his boldness, but Sir Charles only laughed gently.

"Oh, yes, they do," he said. "We tell them often enough in our books and our medical papers. But they see the aim, my dear Jenkins, unlike you I am afraid. They see how noble, how important our work is. They see how important, how immensely valuable, how necessary it is, in fact, to humanity, to know that monkeys can have measles!" he broke off laughing and Jenkins felt again the big man was making fun of him. Sir Charles did not seem to mind now being late for church. He was amused at the poor simple ignorant fellow before him and he liked the feeling that he could confuse him with his big words and twist him round his finger.

Jenkins stood blinking for a moment in silence. The little spaniel's agonised moaning came from the room behind him and filled his ears making a curious undertone to the light banter of the man before him. Sir Charles was a great believer in propaganda and never let go an opportunity of sowing the good seed. He was a little afraid that sooner or later an infuriated populace might turn against him and his colleagues and put a stop to those practices for which now they so meekly and conveniently paid: so seeing Jenkins still appeared somewhat obdurate he continued more seriously.

"Just think a minute. There's the whole country! England! You love England, don't you, Jenkins? Fought for it, eh?"

"Yes, Sir, I do," replied Jenkins fervently. His whole face lighted up.

"Well, now England's in the forefront of all humanitarian projects. Won't have bull fights, stopped cock fights, sends men to prison for throwing a cat out of a window, would *England* allow this work of ours to go on, if it were cruel? No she would stop it. Would she tax her people to give us little gifts of 500,000 pounds for Research if it were cruel? Certainly not. Are you a taxpayer, Jenkins?"

"I must be, Sir. We're all taxed."

"Just so. Then here in the laboratory you'll have the satisfaction of seeing how your money is spent for you. Money, Jenkins, it takes money, the noble work. Sixty thousand animals more or less go through the laboratories every year in England. Expensive ones too, some of them: it takes money, *your* money, see?" Here the doctor gave his victim a playful little dig in the side. "Now I really must run off. Don't you bother your head about these things. Just remember what I say that England's a splendidly humane country and couldn't allow anything brutal to be done and don't forget too how awfully important it is to know that monkeys have measles!"

Before his confused listener could make any remark the doctor had walked down the passage, passed through the door and banged it behind him.

Sir Charles walked down the road and across the straggling bit of waste ground that surrounded his laboratory, with a pleased expression on his face. One of his favorite experiments was to batter a dog to death slowly with repeated blows, making notes during the operation, of the time necessary to produce insensibility and the further time to produce actual extinction. It was always an interesting experiment to his highly scientific mind and he felt in some degree as if he had been practicing in the same way on Jenkins' mind. He thought with a

77

smile it would not take long in his laboratory to batter to death all Jenkins' funny little ideas about cruelty.

Jenkins, left standing in the hall, remained there as if transfixed. He felt as if the whole thing must be some horrible nightmare and that he would wake up in a minute in his country cottage with the sound of clucking hens outside, instead of that awful moaning from the room behind him.

What sort of hell was this that he had dropped into?

You see Jenkins lacked a scientific education which enables a man to see that black is really white and so on. Jenkins was only just an average ordinary man so he must be excused if Sir Charles' most beautifully kept and perfectly appointed laboratory with all the latest scientific appliances for giving monkeys measles and kindred noble work, appeared to him a hell.

How had he got into it?

Seeing by chance that scrap of paper and the advertisement that a man was wanted to take charge of animals, he had applied for the place, because he was fond of animals, and got it.

He had arrived last night and been shown his quarters. He had also been shown a room with four healthy happy dogs in it in kennels round the walls. He had been told to feed them and keep them clean which work he had joyfully accepted. The dogs had jumped round him in delight recognizing a friend and he had spent most of his evening with them, cleaning out the kennels which seemed to be old ones that had been used for many occupants before these four had been put into them. His work done he had passed through a passage with closed doors on all sides of him and up the long flight of stairs at the end of it, to his own two rooms, on an upper floor. These seemed cosy enough and he had slept well. In the early morning he had been roused by the unearthly screaming of a dog and fearing some accident had happened to one of his charges, he bolted down to the room where he had left them overnight.

Finding only three scared looking animals there, he had followed the terrible scream down the passage, opened the door that faced him and come straight in on the scene of one of the doctor's scientific operations. Jenkins being unscientific failed to see any trace of beauty and nobleness in the work before him. He only saw a perspiring man in a blood stained smock holding a dog who was shrieking like a human person in the extreme of pain and terror. He understood nothing, he vaguely thought there must be some accident and his help was needed.

He rushed forward. "Oh, Sir—"

The scientist looked up. His face was working, his eye glaring.

"Damn you, you fool, what do you come here for when I'm at work? Get out. Get out!" he repeated as Jenkins did not stir. "And never come here unless I ring for you."

Jenkins turned on shaking legs and got out of the room somehow, shutting the door tightly behind him. Then he walked down the passage to the room where the live dogs were, entered and shut that door too and stood with his back against it facing his charges. Yesterday they had jumped up to him. Now they stood still, looking at him askance. Their ears pricked listening to those frightful screams. Then he went into the middle of the room and sat down on a wooden chair and buried his face in his hands with a groan. He couldn't yet make much head or tail of it all but one thing was certain. The man in the other room was cutting up a dog alive. A dog who had been well and happy last night. It had been taken from among these out of this room and by inference these others were awaiting the same fate. And they knew it: he stretched out his hands to them and after a time they came up to him; not as last night capering and joyous, but cowering and whimpering, sidling up to him pleading for a protection they felt by instinct he could not give. He had put his arms round them and so they sat grouped together the man and the terrified dogs listening to those horrible cries. He did not know how long he sat there but after a time a church bell clanged out a few harsh strokes and after that the doctor's bell had sounded summoning him to his duties. Now the great man had departed and he was left in the hallway to think over his first lesson in applied Science.

Jenkins was not an educated man, but he had a good clear mind capable of adjusting itself to new situations. He was, besides, what we all understand by a good man. He had those simple sincere rules of conduct that make the useful citizen. He had his own very definite ideas of right and wrong and lived up to them. He thought it was right to pay your way, to help your neighbour whenever possible, to work hard and mind your own business. He thought it wrong to lie, steal or murder, to cheat or injure another in any way, or to abuse the helpless and the weak. That was his simple code and it had served him very well the 38 years of his hard-working life. He saw now chance had flung him into a place where what seemed to him scandalous infamies were carried on and his first impulse was to flee from it, as one would from any plague spot: make a clean bolt of it and forget that such a place existed. But he checked the impulse as cowardly. No, here he was suddenly up against something he did not in the least understand. It was his duty to try to master it and see what it all meant. He perceived very clearly that however gross the evil existing here it was one legally protected and upheld. He remembered he had once called in a policeman to stop a man beating a dog: nothing of that sort would avail here, that was evident. The doctor was quite confident and easy in his mind apparently and while the exterior of the place looked squalid and desolate situated in its ragged waste land, the interior was fitted up with every comfort and even luxury. Electric lights and lamps and telephones were in every room he had seen. Beyond the outlying position, there seemed no special secrecy or concealment about the place: No: somehow or other, he could not think how, but *somehow* this man was *allowed* to do what he was doing. Allowed as he had said, by the country, by the laws, by the church, by his fellows, to do these atrocities. His blood boiled within him. Again came the temptation to bolt but the thought of the animals held him. His fighting spirit was up but he could do nothing until he knew more about what sort of a hell he was in. He must explore. He walked down the softly carpeted hallway away from the door, towards the staircase end and opening the first door he came to at the side entered the apartment. It was long and narrow. No carpet here: on the floor only bare tessellated black and white tiles. There were windows high up in the walls: below these ranged against each side of the room were iron cages. The light fell coldly from above and there was a faint foul odour in the air that belied the appearance of aggressive brightness and cleanliness of the whole place. There was a row of iron cages on each side all down the long room and from these rose a continuous low moaning sound which seemed to chill his blood. He looked at the cages: each one was occupied by a mutilated or diseased animal: most of them turning, swaying and moaning in direst agony in their cramped quarters: others crouching motionless with staring eyes, frozen images of despair. Jenkins turned to the first cage on his right. It contained a retriever blinded in both eyes from the sockets of which oozed blood and matter. He was sitting on his haunches on the bare iron floor of his cage in which he could just turn round, that was all: the bars at the top almost touched his head.

Jenkins stopped and spoke gently to him. The dog raised his ears a little at the unaccustomed sound and threw up his great gentle glossy head with the most piteous long drawn howl that Jenkins had ever heard. Its accent of unutterable woe was such that no human voice could achieve. It said as plainly as words, "Oh, let me out of my prison house, let me die and escape."

Jenkins eyes filled. He spoke again and put his hand through the bars and stroked the dog's shoulder and the sightless face turned towards his hand and the dog's hot nose pushed into it with another long drawn pleading howl.

Jenkin's looked at the little white enamelled tablet beneath the cage and read:

"March 1st—Eyes removed." The date was a fortnight back! With a sickening feeling half benumbing him, Jenkins passed to the next cage. Here was a ghastly creature that once had been a dog, staring with glaring eyes through the bars. It took no notice. It's agony appeared to be so appalling that it was mute and rigid with it.

Jenkins stooped and read:

"Tumour (artificial) on brain. Experiment commenced February 15." The next cage held a small spaniel puppy with a hugely bloated body that was twisting and writhing in every conceivable position. It's tongue was hanging out, foam was pouring from its mouth, its eyes bulging from its head, it gave short scream of agony at intervals and threw itself against the bars of its cage.

Jenkins felt it was not mad. Out of the large protruding brown eyes looked not insanity: only terror and wonder at its own awful suffering.

Jenkins read on the cage:

"Virus introduced into stomach." There was no date.

In the next cage the occupant lay at the point of death. It was a small dog: the floor of its cage was one pool of blood. Where one of its ears should have been gaped a huge hole from which blood was still running. Its head had been apparently bandaged. Its paws evidently tied together but in its madness of pain it had torn away its bonds. Now it lay still on its side. Its mouth open gasping, its eyes staring, too weak to move or cry. *Dying at last.*

Jenkins read:

"Ear removed. New ear grafted. February 1st."

A month and a half it had been there!

Jenkins crept on down the middle path between the row: feeling weak and cold as he went. Each cage seemed to him more horrible than the last. Of some the contents are indescribable. Beneath some ran the legend—"Starving Experiments." And in these the dogs lay rough-haired, motionless, their bones almost through their skin, their eyes glazed and the dates ranged from January.

After the dog cages came cats, cats and kittens in all stages of mutilation with their small red tongues showing in their gasping mouths that let out faint little cries for mercy. After these, monkeys and here underneath Jenkins read:

Measles induced at various early dates.

He paused here looking at the suffering creatures, shivering and crouching on the bare zinc floors of their cells and his face grew strangely dark as he recalled the scientist's smiling words: "It's so beneficial to humanity to know that monkeys can have measles!"

His feet crept on again. He felt he could hardly move them but he determined to see it all. Other monkeys had suffered such frightful injuries he could hardly recognize what they were. Their wizened anguished little faces were pressed against the bars. They clung there whining and chattering. Some without eyes, some without ears, some with huge lumps in their throats that they continually pulled at with trembling paws. Then the cages ended. He had come to the end of the row and he saw in front of him a round zinc cylinder-shaped receptacle, just like in appearance the ash barrels seen in back yards. He noticed, however, this had perforated holes in the lid. He lifted this off and down at the bottom of the barrel lay a collie dog.

He called to it and it lifted its head apathetically and gazed up with dull eyes. It was very, very emaciated: just its coat seemed covering its skeleton. Jenkins put down both his arms into the barrel and very gently lifted the dog out bodily and set it on the ground. It lay just where he set it, crumpled up. Then he raised it and spoke to it. The dog apparently tried to respond and moved but as it got on its feet it turned and turned and turned in an endless awful circle. It could not do otherwise. Its head bent down at a queer angle, its legs quivering, its tail and ears hanging, its eyes lifeless, its bones sticking in places through its rough hair, it turned and turned on the same small spot of ground till it sank exhausted.

Jenkins read:

"Portion of brain removed. Interesting circular movement induced." And the date was *two years before the present time*.

Jenkins straightened himself, the distorted creature crouching, silent at his feet.

"And this is *England*!" he said half aloud.

Impossible to cure, to help, to alleviate any of this suffering. Impossible to bestow the last boon of death on these sad helpless beings. For if he freed any of these, new ones would be put in their place.

With his heart heaving, and beating in a tumult of fury, he bent and very tenderly lifted the skeleton collie in his arms, held it for a moment against him and spoke to it gently. Then lowered it back into its awful prison house and replaced the lid.

Then shivering as if with mortal cold he dragged himself on a few paces to the end of the room where there was a small gas fire burning and an arm chair drawn up by it. He sank into this and put his hands to the fire. This was the doctor's end of the apartment. A screen shut it off from the long line of cages. A square of warm carpet covered the bare tiles on the floor. A small table with some paper and-note books and a shaded lamp stood in front of the fire. Jenkins sat in the doctor's chair listening to the moaning of unspeakable pain that filled all the air, low and desolate and hopeless, and shuddered.

When the feeling of physical illness had worn off a little, he rose to his feet and retraced his steps down the long avenue of cages. He could not bear to look at them again but kept his gaze resolutely in front of him. He knew he could do nothing to help the hapless tortured inmates. His duties were to clean out the cages and to feed and water and wait upon the healthy animals. He was not allowed to interfere with the animals under experiment. If he overstepped his limit by the very least he saw he would be thrown out at once and he was bent upon staying. He felt quite clearly he was face to face with some momentous evil that was vast and far-reaching and of which he could not read the meaning. He could not grapple with it for he did not fully yet understand what it was but he would be patient, he would be calm, he would be self-controlled, he would watch and study and wait and then perhaps he could do something. But infinite caution would be necessary: no rash step, no giving way to raging impulses of anger and indignation would serve him here nor help those tortured prisoners. "Who sups with the devil must have a long spoon" and he felt he was now the guest of the devil, indeed.

He got out of the apartment at last and closed the door after him. He went down the hallway and listened at the small laboratory door behind which he knew the dog was lying clamped in the trough. The moaning had ceased. There was no sound now. Jenkins crept on up the stairs to his own top floor rooms. Before commencing the flight he first noticed another door on his left which he had not opened. He read on it in passing on a small plate, Lethal Chamber. He dragged himself up the stairs and finally reached his own little rooms at the top: with which he had been so pleased the night before. Only the night before and it seemed he had lived through an age of misery since then. He entered his own little sitting room, bolted the door after him and then sat down at the table, his head in his hands, a broken man. His beliefs, faiths, ideals, were all shattered and fell from him leaving him naked and alone.

This was England; These things were done in England, allowed, approved of, and he had loved England, believed in it, fought for it. Did he love it now? No. Would he fight for it and offer his life again for it? No. He had believed in God. He had loved him. Not all the war and the suffering and the horror of it had shaken his belief in Him. Did he believe in Him now? Love Him? No. There could be no loving, good, all-powerful being who could look down on that laboratory and that man who worked there and not shrivel them both to nothing. A

God there might be, but if these things pleased Him then He must be evil. If they did not please Him He must be as powerless as Jenkins himself to stop them.

Perhaps it was that. Perhaps there was a spirit of good but perhaps it could not work alone, perhaps it needed human co-operation. This was a new thought to Jenkins and it give a little light to the broken and dejected man.

CHAPTER 2

Day after day went slowly by and Jenkins toiled along the painful road of life into which he had been so suddenly brought, bearing his burden of grief and pain and learning, learning all the time. Every hour he saw further into and through the mist of horror that surrounded him. He learnt greedily. He felt it was vitally necessary to learn everything about this terrible wrong that he saw being committed, if he wished in any way to remedy it. To fight a thing successfully you must know what it is: you must know what you are fighting.

He saw many volumes on the doctor's bookshelves and asked permission to read them which was genially accorded him.

"You'll find things to stagger you in them," Sir Charles said pleasantly, "and lots of hard words. I don't think you'll get very far with them." But Jenkins did get much farther than the doctor thought. He found the books were mostly volumes written by scientific men describing their own work, records of experiments they had made on living animals set out in full by themselves. And in spite of the stupid jargon of words surrounding them and the heavy language Jenkins saw that two things stood out very plainly, one, the hideous suffering of the animals thus used, the other the absolute uselessness and senselessness of the experiments as far as regarded Humanity. They were very enlightening books and so Jenkins found them. Then there was a big scrap book compiled by the doctor himself, that led Jenkins far along the road of understanding. This book contained newspaper cuttings of all descriptions bearing in any way on medical life and work.

Reports of coroners' inquests especially those where the conduct of a doctor or nurse had been called in question and where invariably they had been triumphantly cleared by the coroner (usually himself a doctor) and votes of sympathy extended to them. These passages had been underscored with a red pencil and often a note of exclamation added to them, by the old cynic who had pasted them in. There were many announcements of wonderful cures and these were starred by a blue pencil and many pages further on in cuttings of a later date Jenkins would find these "cures" contradicted and dismissed as worthless hoaxes and a blue star was put against these also. Then there were long panegyrics on medical science in general and underneath these were mostly pencilled notes by the doctor, "Written by Smith," "Good old Ted," "Very good Charlie," "That's the stuff to give 'em," and so on. Then there were pictures of Royalty opening hospital wards: Royalty going to balls in aid of hospitals, etc., and side by side with these, accounts of patients who had jumped from hospital windows: patients who had died on the operating table, patients who having lost their limbs or their sight by the mistreatment in hospitals went back to their garrets to hang themselves or gas themselves to death. Sometimes these columns were marked by exclamation marks, some times the juxtaposition was left to speak for itself. Jenkins could just imagine the face of the doctor with his tongue in his cheek, as he glued the cuttings in.

Jenkins spent many hours hanging fascinated over this volume.

From the vivisectors' own books he learnt what vivisection really was, from the reports in the papers he learnt what the public thought it was and how they were assiduously taught by the press to regard it and medical science generally.

Then there were other means of self education, one of the best of which though the most painful was listening to the doctor's conversation and that of his friends on those evenings when the great man had some friends or some young students in to visit him. Jenkins would be called upon to wait on them at a light supper with heavy drinks which they took in the doctor's study.

Jenkins as has been said was not a scientific person, he was simply a man of common sense and the way those scientific men talked, the utter brutality and callousness of their jokes, their stories, their whole view of the sufferings of humanity, the confessions they made or rather perhaps one should say the boasts, of how they had acted in their hospital wards, made his blood run cold.

One thing he saw, emerged very clearly and restored somewhat to his mind the belief in eternal Justice. He saw that this Scientific Research, so unutterably wicked and cruel to the animals, was at the same time proving an unspeakable curse to humanity.

As he heard the talk of reckless experiments on patients unnecessary operations, over-doses of X-ray that burnt human insides out, and the joking and laughter over human agony, he recognized that Humanity was being justly punished and that the men, degraded by horrible experiments on animals were totally unfitted to have the care of sick and helpless men and women.

One night climbing to his room after attendance at one of these suppers and listening to the revolting talk, he went to bed, white and dizzy and shaking. In the darkness and stillness a question seemed to form itself within him and he examined it carefully bringing all the knowledge he had gained to bear upon it.

Ought he to kill this man?

Murder! That would be murder: a horrible idea, a horrible thought, a horrible word to the well-balanced, civilized mind; and to Jenkins, sober and straight-living, the typical good citizen without a trace of criminality in his disposition it was appalling.

Murder! No! On no account must one murder. It was an essentially wrong, unpardonable act. But would it be murder? he asked himself in his clear, hard-thinking though uneducated mind. Would it not be justifiable homicide? Let him consider. He must consider this question from all points. Here he was on the verge of a decision to commit an act forbidden by the law of his country, regarded with detestation by his fellows and condemned by religion. He would take the point of law first. The law allowed justifiable homicide. If that were the verdict, the accused was acquitted with honour.

On what grounds was that verdict given when one man killed another? First, self-defence. If the doctor attacked him and he feared his own life was in danger, he might kill the doctor with impunity. *His own life.* He might kill the doctor to save his own life.

Then why not to save something he valued much more highly? To save from agonising suffering those thousand of helpless innocent loving animals that the doctor would torture during his evil life? *Jenkins' life*, what was that? Like all brave natures he had hardly a thought for it. A run-away horse, a woman in a canal, a child on a railway track, any of these might call for and receive its sacrifice at any time. Certainly to save even that one line of animals in the laboratory, slowly perishing in their long drawn out anguish he would have laid down his life, had that been able to help matters.

Therefore, if the law allowed him to murder to save his own life, why should it not allow him to murder to save something he valued infinitely more? Jenkins revolved this anxiously and slowly in his sedate mind till he came to the conclusion that the law should permit him this choice.

Then he took up another point: the law would certainly call it justifiable homicide if he saw the doctor murdering a man, woman or child, any human being, even an imbecile, and killed him in defence of any of those. Then why should he not kill him to save those thousands of poor patients that the doctor would certainly murder if allowed to live out his evil life to its natural close? Only that evening he had heard him saying to a student that he had performed a certain operation three thousand times and it had never done any good: only killed or crippled. Jenkins shuddered as he thought of the mutilated victims dragging out their ruined lives; women who had come to the doctor full of hope and faith and had been sent away according to his own statement, shattered wrecks. *But what could they expect?* How could they come to a man for sympathy or expect him to be moved or restrained by any decent feeling when he spent his whole life wallowing in the most frightful mutilation of animals?

Jenkins marvelled at their folly.

But he must get back to his point as to the law. The law would allow him to kill the doctor if he were murdering *one* woman, then why not when he was murdering thousands? Again, there was that paragraph in a daily paper stating that a certain serum had been "successfully tried on 300 children." What about all the children on whom it had been unsuccessfully "tried"?

Jenkins seemed for a moment to see round him a plain covered with the small graves of children, done to death by the modern Moloch—Science. He would save the lives of many human victims as well as the animal victims if he extinguished this one evil existence.

Since Jenkins had come to the laboratory he had not seen one single useful experiment made, one single operation that might be excused by some people on the ground of its utility. He had seen cats filled with water till they burst, of what good is that to humanity? He had seen dogs distorted by rickets, and dogs put into boxes which were gradually heated while the doctor watched the animals inside through a glass window panting and writhing without water or air. He had seen the dogs dragged out in a desperate condition and expire within half an hour. How was humanity benefited? He had seen monkeys suffering cruelly from measles, to what end? He had seen animals covered with tar expiring in lingering agonies. What was the use?

He had seen the doctor take a clear eyed, healthy cat and deliberately induce an ulcer in one eye and watch it day by day, eating the organ away and when the work of destruction was complete he would set up an ulcer in the other eye, encouraged apparently rather than the reverse by its heartrending screams of pain and finally throw it back into its cage in total blindness and convulsions of agony. And the results? What had the Scientists to show?

A few of their vaunted remedies passed in review before him:

Insulin which the Scientists admitted amongst themselves to be more deadly than the diabetes it was supposed to cure.

Anti-toxin for diphtheria, dangerous and unknown as to its after effects while the simple Bella Donna was a known specific for the disease. The inoculation of anti-typhoid serum used in the war. Jenkins had been to the war and he knew that where the sanitation had been good, there had been no typhoid. Where the sanitation had been bad the anti-typhoid serum had not saved the troops. Typhoid had reigned in spite of it. And so on, and so on. In the whole long list of "discoveries" and "remedies" emanating from laboratories there was not one that he could find that had been proved of benefit, not one for which a simple common-sense substitute could not be found.

Useful, beneficial, good—any of this work? No, it was simply hellish and having seen it as he had at close quarters and recognising it for what it was, it was his duty to stop it in the only way he could.

It would not be murder, it would be homicide and justifiable a hundred times over.

Anger carried him away for a moment but he brought his thoughts back to calm consideration. What good would it do? The removal of this one man? Very little, he admitted sorrowfully. But it seemed to him, in the phrase of the war: "it was his bit."

How often in the recruiting days the men had been told they were not to worry over the larger aspects, the greater issues of the war. They were not to say to themselves that the little which each man could do would not either win or lose the war. No, each man was to do "his bit." If he killed one German it was good. If he killed ten, it was better. And if he shrank from killing a fellow man he was to remember that by so doing he was saving the lives of perhaps hundreds of his comrades.

The same reasoning seemed to apply here. He could not do much. He could not sweep away that cancer of modern civilization—medical scientific research. He could not influence the ending of it, any more than he could influence the ending of the war, but he could do his bit. He could kill this one man and by so doing save thousands of his fellow human beings and thousands of his no less fellow beings—the animals.

The human beings, really, Jenkins doubted if it were his mission to save. If they could be so blind, so stupid, so selfish and so cruel as to allow such work as the doctor's, because they fancied they might gain something from it, it was only Divine Justice that they should be poisoned by the medicines manufactured so hideously. That the Insulin gained by the torture of dogs; the anti-toxins brought by the agony of horses; the small-pox vaccine scooped from the aching sores of cows and all the other vile and filthy products of the laboratory should give them death and disease instead of the relief they sought.

But for the sake of the animals, entirely innocent, unselfish, trusting, devoted, that this fiend would torture daily, year by year, if he lived, for their sake, Jenkins would "do his bit" and save them.

The next morning he rose, his head clear, his heart stout and determined. He had been sent there for some good reason and he seemed to see it clearly before him as Joan of Arc saw her mission revealed to her.

Possessing himself in patience, he would watch and wait till the opportunity came to take the doctor's life and then he would take it as Jael slew Sisera, as Judith slew Holofernes. How many lives had he taken in the war? He could not remember but it must have been many: lives of good honest brave men fighting for their country as he was fighting for his, then should he hesitate now to take a life so mean, so worthless, so harmful not only to his fellow creatures the animals but also to his fellow men? Why should he not rid the world of this monster? A great calmness fell upon Jenkins as he made his resolve and from that hour, though he lived in pain, he had the courage lent him, of a man devoted to a cause.

CHAPTER 3

It was a Saturday evening and an evil-looking man stood at the door, when Jenkins opened it to a modest ring. He had a large black bag which bulged and looked heavy in his hand.

"A fine cat, mister," he whispered hoarsely, "only two bob, hand over and let me go."

Jenkins took the bag and loosening the string at its mouth looked down into it. At the bottom was a soft mass of handsome-looking fur from which a faint mew came as the cat saw Jenkins' face at the top of the bag. It was evidently very tame and nestled up against Jenkins' chest directly he drew it out. It was a magnificent creature, not a Persian, but with a very thick coat, pure white and a tail like the brush of an Arctic fox. Jenkins returned the bag and gave two shillings to the man with the evil face who immediately melted into the darkness and Jenkins was just closing the door, the cat still in his arms, when the doctor came up from the outside and entered.

"That's a fine animal," he remarked as he closed the door and the cat turned its great golden eyes on him, "how much did you have to give?"

"Only 2/ Sir," Jenkins answered, "the man has stolen it I should think."

The doctor laughed.

"Evidently. Some old maid's cat, I expect. Nice tame beast," he put his hand on the cat's head and ruffled the fur backwards and forwards rather roughly. The cat put its head back and looked at the doctor with some resentment in its golden eyes. "Accustomed to sit on the table and drink cream out of the old maid's saucer, eh?" he went on half playfully. "Well, we've a little table here for you, my beauty. We'll set you on it and clamp you down and then we set it spinning. One hundred miles an hour or more we keep you whirling round for a fortnight and then when we take you off your eyes will be all criss-cross and you'll be just mad with terror. That's what we'll do with you, Pussy." Then he walked on humming into his own study, into which he went and slammed the door. Jenkins left standing in the passage, the cat still clasped to him, wondered whether men were men or fiends. A sick loathing grew up in him and seemed to submerge his spirit like a great wave. Then it rolled over, leaving him with a clear fierce determination that come what might, this thing in his arms so gentle, so trustful, should never be placed on that hellish table.

The cat, distressed by something in the doctor's touch or voice or face, turned its head up to Jenkins and fixed its beautiful golden gaze on him and apparently from Jenkins' drawn sad face it gained confidence and began to purr. Jenkins with the fire of hatred glowing in his heart against mankind climbed the stairs to his own room and deposited the cat on his bed. He then set his stove going, drew his curtains and poured out a saucer of milk. The cat watched all these proceedings appreciatively and purred loudly in response. When it had lapped up all the milk while Jenkins held the saucer, it lay back on the bed and stretched its paws up purring, saying quite clearly, "Come and caress me, I'm accustomed to it. I'm a very nice cat," and Jenkins sat beside it, stroking it, with the tears burning behind his eye-lids. It was a stolen pet evidently and Jenkins would not have taken it in at the door except that he knew if he refused it, where possibly through him it might have a chance of safety, the cat stealer would simply take it on to another accursed laboratory where it would have *no* chance of escape from the tortures awaiting it.

That night the doctor called to Jenkins as he was going up to bed, "I'm very busy just now. I've got so many things going to attend to but I'll have more time in a week or so. Just remind me about the cat later on, will you? If I forget."

Jenkins listened, his face growing dark as he stood in the shadow, on the stairs.

"Yes, Sir," he replied and went on up.

The cat was waiting for him curled on the bed and mewed delightedly at his entrance, showing its white teeth and its little pink tongue, curled up like a rose leaf, behind them.

Jenkins seated himself beside the cat and fed it on some scraps he had brought up with him. For a week the cat remained, a willing prisoner in his room. He gave it a large tray of earth over by the window to scratch in and replenished it every day from the bit of common ground round the house. He brought everything up to it and waited on it and never let it out where evil eyes could fall on it and all that week he searched the papers daily for some announcement of a lost cat. There were no shops very near the laboratory but he walked every day to the nearest, a small newsagent's and tobacconist's where he bought his papers and then studied them diligently in his own room.

At last he found the notice he wanted.

"Lost. A large white tomcat. Not Persian, but thick coat and bushy tail. Finder will be handsomely rewarded if he brings cat to blank Grosvenor Square, W."

Jenkins read this with a beating heart. This was his cat he felt sure. The doctor was away for his usual week end. This was Saturday. He always was allowed Sunday afternoon for himself. To-morrow he would take the cat back to its owner.

That night he held it tightly to him and hardly slept but spent his time stroking and caressing it and realising how lonely he would be without it. But still to get it out of this hell, safe and alive, was everything. The cat, with all its claws sheathed in its velvet skin patted gently with its paws Jenkins' thin cheeks and nestled close to him purring ecstatically. It missed its own house and mistress but no animal could be insensible of the flood of love and sympathy that poured out from Jenkins' unhappy heart. The next morning he spent much time on brushing and combing its silky coat and about two in the afternoon with his heart high in hope he set out for Grosvenor Square, the cat curled round in the lidded basket which Jenkins had brought, filled with vegetables, with him from the country. He thought if he; could once see the owner of the cat and tell him or her of the horrors his or her pet had so narrowly escaped, then surely anyone so rich and powerful as to be able to live in Grosvenor Square would take some steps against the system which made these horrors possible.

When he arrived at the door of the house it was opened by a footman who at once glanced at the basket. When Jenkins asked to see the person who had put in the advertisement, the man replied affably, "Miss Courtneidge is in and I think will see you." Then he stooped down and scratched at the basket side. "Cushy," he called and a mew of recognition came from within.

"Come upstairs," he said and Jenkins followed full of joyful anticipation of coming face to face with someone who surely would listen to his message. He entered a large room and at the far end there sat Miss Courtneidge, a fat, middle-aged woman with a bright intelligent and pleasing face. She jumped up and took the basket from Jenkins smiling and lifted the lid.

"Oh, there you are Cushy," she exclaimed, and lifted the creature out with many murmurs of delight.

Jenkins stood by respectfully enjoying the scene to the full. There was no doubt the lady genuinely loved her pet and the cat could hardly have a better mistress.

"Do sit down," she said after a minute, "and tell me where you found him."

She sat down with the cat in her arms and Jenkins took a seat opposite her.

"A man, a regular cat stealer, I think, brought him in a bag to our place and offered him to me for 2/—I saw at once he was stolen and I thought I'd better take him and try to find the owner. If I hadn't, the man would have taken him to another laboratory where they wouldn't have bothered to restore him to his owner but used him in the laboratory."

The lady was listening intently to Jenkins and he thought her eyes grew harder.

"What are you then?" she asked quietly.

"I am an attendant at a laboratory for Scientific Research," returned Jenkins, "and the man brought the cat to be experimented upon, but I don't like the business and I meant to save this cat anyway."

"If you don't like it, why do you stay?" asked the lady quietly and very coldly.

Jenkins realised that his hearer's sympathies were alienated from him and the false position in which he stood came home to him. At first he had thought it might be possible to make a clean breast of his feelings. He had visions of the lady coming to see the tortured animals and in her righteous wrath having the hideous place done away with altogether, but now something in the coldness of her voice and eyes warned him he must go very carefully.

"I stay to try and do what I can for the animals," he answered, "do you know about this Scientific Research, ma'am?"

"I know that it is a very noble work carried on by selfless men and women who give up their lives to the cause of humanity," replied the lady proudly.

Jenkins looked back at her aghast as these parrot phrases fell from her lips. Evidently she knew nothing at all about it and against this dense ignorance he felt he had no weapons.

"You don't know what goes on in the laboratories, animals are tortured to death and given the most hideous sufferings that don't lead to anything," he said.

The lady compressed her lips.

"I can't believe you," she said icily, "I have many friends who are doctors and scientific men and I am sure they would do nothing but what is right. If they have to experiment on animals I am sure they do it kindly."

Jenkins could have laughed bitterly as he heard but he controlled himself and answered:

"How *can* you starve animals kindly, ma'am?"

The lady looked cross and was silent for a moment and Jenkins burst out:

"Do come with me now and I'll show you what Scientific Research really means. The laboratory is empty, I am in sole charge, the doctor is away. Come and see the animals for yourself. Then you can judge about it."

The lady looked crosser than ever.

"Thank you. I am quite capable of judging the matter already. I rely upon what my doctor tells me. In any case, if there were any cruelty, I couldn't bear to see it, I couldn't sleep for a week if I did."

Again Jenkins felt helpless and appalled. What stupendous folly, what selfishness! Any cruelty might be practiced, provided *she* did not see it, provided *her* sleep was not disturbed.

"I really must ask you to go now," she continued. "I have a meeting this afternoon here of the League of Love. We have the Bishop coming and we are going to organize something to aid the hospitals."

Jenkins rose immediately.

"To aid the hospitals! To build new laboratories for the torture of *more* animals! Oh ma'am, you don't know what you are doing! If *I* had not saved your cat he'd have been pinned down to an electric table and spun round at 100 miles an hour for a fortnight and taken off it mad and blind to have his brain opened and looked at. That was *his* fate and how does that help humanity?"

The lady was standing too.

"You need not expect that I shall increase your reward for bringing him back by telling me these wicked stories," she said severely. "Here is two pounds. I shall not give you any more!" and she held towards him two pound-notes.

Over Jenkins' face ran a flame of scarlet, then faded leaving him ashy white. That was what she thought! That he was detailing false sufferings to increase his own reward!

He took the notes from her hand and dropped them on the floor and then stepped forward and put his foot down on them, looking her full in the face.

"That, ma'am, is what I care for your reward! I brought that creature back to you because I loved it. I never thought of the reward and should not have taken any in any case. I pray some day you may be shaken out of the darkness and the ignorance you live in."

He turned and strode to the door, leaving the notes on the floor and the lady too astonished to say anything. A pair of golden eyes watched him depart and a little soft mew came to his ears as he closed the door and seemed to stab into his heart.

He walked down the stairs and out into the street with a sorely wounded spirit. All the joy and elation at having rescued the cat and restored it was blotted out by the cold tide of despair. He felt that he was helpless to save others just as loving, just as beautiful as this one, from death by torture. What could he do? So long as the world consisted of the friends who did these things and the fools who were so kind that they couldn't believe in the fiends and so cowardly that they would not consider the question for fear of losing a night's sleep, what could he do? "God help me, God help me," was the cry that rose in his heart. And formerly it had comforted him and he had believed that God would help him however unkind man might be. But how? Was there any God? Was it not a Devil who ruled the world if this sort of Scientific Research were allowed in it? Why should God help him, if he cared nothing for the miseries of the innocent and sweet animals he had created?

Thoroughly miserable he went back to the hell on the common and up in his own room, making his solitary tea, he took himself severely to task. Had he wasted that golden opportunity, when he, knowing the truth, was face to face with one who knew nothing except some phrases culled from the articles of doctors, in the Press? Could he have done better? Was it his fault that he had failed? Over and over in his mind he turned that conversation but could decide nothing. His brains felt battered and weary but he was glad the cat was gone.

The very next morning when the doctor returned, he called Jenkins into his study.

"Jenkins our stock of dogs is low, isn't it?"

"The last one died last night, Sir."

"Oh: which was that?"

"The little Skye you were starving, Sir."

"H'm: when did I begin? Do you remember?"

"Ten days ago."

"Ten days! That's quite a good record. Isn't it? Had it eaten that coke I put in the cage?"

"No, Sir. Only gnawed it a bit. I found blood on it where the coke had cut its mouth. It hadn't eaten it."

"Oh, well," cheerily, "we must get in some more dogs. By the way, there's that cat, bring me that."

"Sorry, Sir, the cat escaped."

"What?" the doctor wheeled round in his chair and looked piercingly at his attendant, but Jenkin's face was still and stolid as a mask.

"You let it go, you mean, do you? I thought you were rather soft headed over that cat when it came in. Now look here, mind this, if any more animals *escape* at any time, I shall have no further use for you. See?"

"Yes, Sir."

"And to-morrow morning you'll go and get me half a dozen kittens: big ones. Go to the Army and Navy Stores or anywhere you like but mind those kittens are here by noon. I am going to try some eye transplanting."

Jenkins withdrew.

How could such a man be allowed to exist, he asked himself. How could such a place as this stand? Why did not a lightning stroke burn it to the ground with its fiendish owner inside? Why did not the flame that swept over Sodom and Gomorra sweep also over the laboratories of London and obliterate them?

Then he smiled grimly remembering how the laboratories were supported by the tax payer, approved by the king, and beloved by the aristocracy.

What was he, Jenkins, to think differently from all these? He was only a poor common-sense man of the people. But he knew and they did not. That was the tragedy of it. He would have given his life to be able to tell and convince them.

CHAPTER 4

One evening the doctor on coming home tossed a card over to Jenkins with the remark, "Better come to the lecture and hear me talk the money out of the public pocket."

Jenkins looked at the card and saw it admitted him at 8 p. m. on the coming Thursday evening to a lecture on Scientific Research by Sir Charles Smith-Brown, Dsc. M.D., etc., etc. Jenkins thanked him and put the card in his pocket and on the next Thursday he presented his ticket punctually at the time and place appointed.

The small lecture room was already well filled when Jenkins entered and he noticed that the first four or five rows of seats were railed off by a crimson cord from the rest and in these were seated people that Jenkins recognized immediately as "gentlefolk." They were all very well dressed in semi-evening dress and had, for the most part, nice kind-looking intelligent faces. Jenkins spirits rose as he saw them.

"Surely they can't easily be humbugged," he thought, "they've been taught to read and think and had plenty of time for schooling."

He slipped quietly into a vacant seat he saw some rows back of the red cord. Here the people were all in hats and coats and had evidently come on foot to the meeting. Their faces were harder looking than those in front but they also looked intelligent, interested and alert. Jenkins particularly liked the look of his neighbour. A hard working man he should think, perhaps a small tradesman running his own business or perhaps a clerk, anyway he looked keen and quick as a man with his own decided ideas and opinions.

The platform was now filling up with figures: the ladies resplendent in gay coloured Opera cloaks and wearing jewels in their beautifully dressed hair, the men showing large expanses of shirt front. Among these Jenkins noted the sleek form of the doctor and a glow of hatred seemed to spread through him as he noted the suave smile on the thin lips and the benign expression of the whole face so different from the set, savage stare Jenkins was familiar with as the man worked in his laboratory, tearing muscle and nerve out of quivering flesh.

"Blasted hypocrite," he thought furiously to himself and then he noted the eyes of his neighbour quickly passing over the platform as the stately and imposing figures filed onto it quietly and took their appointed seats.

"Who are they all?" he asked in an undertone of the keen faced one.

"Regular swells, all of them," the man returned in the same discreet voice which was quick like his eyes. "That's the Marquis of Sedlestone in the chair and that's Lord and Lord and Lord," he ran off the names so quickly Jenkins could hardly catch them. "He's gulled them all. They all believe in him and this beastly Research. That's what beats me. How they can be such fools."

Jenkins nodded sympathetically. He felt happier. Evidently this man beside him knew the truth of things. He longed intensely to confide in him and tell him what *he* knew but he controlled the impulse. If he was to carry out successfully his great scheme absolute secrecy and concealment of his own feelings was necessary. There was no time for further talk in any case for after a few preliminaries on the platform had been arranged, there was the silver tinkle of a bell and the Marquis of Sedlestone rose to address the audience.

There was absolute silence in the hall and Jenkins listened breathlessly to every word.

"My Lords, ladies and gentlemen, we have the privilege to-night of being gathered together to listen to one of the most distinguished men of our time, Sir Charles Brown-Smith, M.D. Dsc. Science may be said to be the leading force in the world to-day and in him we see one of its most brilliant exponents." (Applause.) "Science to-day is advancing with the steps of a giant. Disease and decay are fading, diminishing, vanishing before it."

"What bosh all that is when they can't cure a common cold," thought Jenkins.

"Maladies are disappearing. Yellow fever is conquered, consumption all but conquered, cancer—"

"Is increasing," shouted a voice at the back of the hall.

There was some laughter in the back seats but only a slight offended rustle from the front rows.

"Alas! Yes," continued the suave well-modulated voice from the platform. "As my friend at the back of the hall has remarked, cancer is increasing and that proves that more research is needed, more patient labour, more funds, more encouragement for those noble men and women who—"

"You've been at it now over twenty years," interrupted the voice in a dominant tone that filled the hall, "and had buckets of money poured into it, without an atom of result, except that cancer is spreading everywhere all the time, and it's you people who are doing it. You're not stopping it: you're spreading it with your beastly laboratories all full of animals dying of it. Aren't they breathing out cancer all the time? Aren't their cages full of it? Aren't the men who look after them carrying cancer germs with them everywhere?"

While these strident questions were being hurled at him, the noble Marquis had waited silent on the platform, looking slightly annoyed and after a second or two he turned and made some observation to a young man sitting behind him, who rose immediately and left the platform by its side door. There had been some applause from various parts of the hall as these questions full of scalding contempt had been shouted out and heads were turned and necks craned to see who the interrupter was. Only the front rows sat unmoved as if they had not heard, their eyes fixed before them waiting for the authorised speaker to continue and a few seconds after the young man had disappeared from the platform, there was a violent scuffle at the back of the room. Between two stout men of the law the interrupter was unceremoniously bundled out.

"There's the Free Speech of England to-day," came a caustic whisper from Jenkins' bright-eyed neighbour, "if ever there's a revolution in England, it'll be these damned medical men who are at the bottom of it."

Jenkins again nodded in silence. The noble Marquis was proceeding.

"As I was saying, Science had made the most remarkable advances and suffering Humanity could turn its eyes hopefully to the future where disease would be stamped out, pain practically abolished, and the onset of old age delayed by 50 or 70 years. But I will not detain you longer. I will leave to our distinguished lecturer the pleasing task of explaining to you how these marvels will be accomplished."

"Awful tosh," murmured keen-eyes as the noble Marquis took his seat and Sir Charles Brown-Smith rose to address the meeting.

"My Lords, ladies and gentlemen," he began, "my noble friend has promised you that I shall tell you some of the most recent marvels Science has accomplished and I will not disappoint you, but first I should like to say a few words on that vexed question—experiments on living animals. Some evilly disposed persons have recently been trying to oppose the glorious march of Science by suggesting that there is cruelty connected with these experiments that are so vital to our work, so necessary to its success, so far reaching in their results for suffering humanity. I wish now to state that in my work I am frequently obliged to resort to these experiments and also to witness them in the studies of others and I can confidently assure you that there is not an atom of cruelty connected with them." Here the doctor paused and beamed upon his docile audience through his large spectacles while a gentle smile suffused his whole benign countenance. A warm murmur of grateful applause rose from the seats beyond the red cord: the mass of the people at the back listened in sullen silence: an indrawn breath of sheer astonishment from Jenkins greeted this stupendous lie.

"The animals," continued the doctor, "who have the honour of being permitted to share in this glorious work, are cared for with devoted attention, no effort is spared in seeing that they are properly housed and well fed. They have every comfort and to see them sporting behind the bars of their spacious cages one would imagine they were rejoicing in their great destiny."

Jenkins, on hearing this, simply turned in his chair, open mouthed to his companion of the keen eyes, and met their clear quizzical gaze fixed upon him.

"Good one, that eh?" keen-eyes murmured.

"Ananias!" shouted an unregenerate person at the back of the hall, "what about your starving experiments?"

The doctor deigned no reply and the former scuffling sounds being repeated, the audience knew that the interrupter had been removed and the English tradition of liberty again upheld.

"Well fed, well cared for, watched over," continued the doctor blandly, "and all they have to suffer is the trifling discomfort of a quick prick from an inoculating needle or a variation of their usual diet."

As these lies poured smoothly forth in the great man's mellow voice, Jenkins saw before him the rows of desolate zinc floored cages, each with its tortured inmate moaning out its life, he saw the puppies starving and distorted beyond recognition in the experiment for rickets, the dog blinded and sitting in hopeless agonies because his eyes had been taken to graft into another dog's sockets, the monkeys wasted to a skeleton or hugely swelled, going blind and semi-paralysed because their thyroid gland had been cut out, all these horrible sights rose before him and he gazed at the speaker, stupefied and dumb.

His neighbour spoke in a low voice in his ear, very low because he had no wish to be turned out. He jerked his thumb in the direction of the red cord.

"Why on earth they don't see that he's guying them, beats me," he said.

"So now let us dismiss this myth of cruelty from our mind, let us remember that great men are rarely cruel and let us refuse to believe these unjust libels that ignorant and prejudiced people are so wantonly spreading." Here the doctor's voice took on a mild severity and the red corders all warmly applauded.

The speaker proceeded.

"I have mentioned how this myth of cruelty impedes the progress of Science but I shall now touch upon something that is even more obstructive to our success: something that is constantly hampering us in our forward march, and that is in this country the absence of compulsion. Yes, my friends, it is true: we are suffering from too much liberty. Liberty is a very excellent thing, a fine thing, but it can be pushed too far, we can have too much of it."

"*Never*," from the back benches.

"Pardon me, we can have too much even of liberty. Liberty which harms ourselves, liberty which harms others must be curtailed. I say unhesitatingly that liberty to refuse the untold benefits of vaccination, of inoculation, is an evil. Those who are so blind as to fail to see the benefits, for themselves, should be forced to accept them. I look forward personally to that time, not I trust, far distant, when like our great sister nation, America, we shall have compulsion for everything that is now left to the ignorant individual to decide for himself."

At this point the red corders began to move uneasily in their chairs and look at each other. They were not quite so sure about all this.

"What can the individual know about the uses or the benefits of the processes offered to him, which he so often rashly and fatally refuses? Is it fair to throw the burden of deciding upon him? How far better that the man of Science, the man who knows, should decide for him and *compel* him to accept the inestimable blessings of Science! I am pleased to say there is a great forward movement to be noticed lately in this direction, no one can enter the Army or the Navy or any public service, nor can a boy go to a public school without being vaccinated for instance, very excellent, very admirable and now that we have the Ministry of Health we may look forward to suitable laws being passed which will bring every individual, no matter of what class or station under the grasp of the healing hand of Science. Personally I think, and I hope, it will not be long before that simple and so necessary operation of taking out the tonsils will be made compulsory."

"I should like to say a word," came a voice from the back and it was so hollow, so sepulchral that it attracted instant attention and even the red corders looked round to see to whom it belonged.

A young man of a pallid countenance and hollow cheeks was standing up and the doctor seeing the audience was interested and would like to hear what the interrupter had to say, affected to be quite willing and waited for him to continue.

"I was well and strong," proceeded the pale cheeked one in his remarkable voice which went all over the hall, "till a medical chap looked down my throat and advised me to have my tonsils cut out. I didn't know what I was in for and went to a hospital and had it done. It's a horrible operation and I suffered for a week after. Well, it's done I think and that's that. But it wasn't over as I thought. My tonsils grow now since they've been cut. In a year I was told they must be done again and now I've been through that damned thing *five times*. I lose a lot of blood each time over it, it gets on my nerves, and I'm a wreck. That's what cutting out tonsils has done for me. And I know it's wrong now. The tonsils are filters put in our throats to filter the air before it reaches the lungs and to stop bad germs going further. I know now what Nature put 'em there for and I say it's a crying shame to take them out."

This last was shouted defiantly and the young man paler than ever before and with beads of sweat standing out on his corpse-like countenance sat down.

There was dead silence for a moment in the hall where Truth for a second had flitted through the fog of lies rising from the platform and rent it with her sharp wings.

Then the doctor, very suave, very smiling, took up his parable again.

"My young friend has indeed suffered and we must extend our sympathies to him. At the same time we must not allow our judgment to be influenced by one unfortunate accidental case, when we know that millions are benefited."

"Who says they are?" shouted back the young man. "Only you doctor people, not those who've been through it!"

"And who should know better than the doctors?" blandly returned the lecturer. "That is just the very point I was going to elaborate when my young friend interrupted me. Perhaps he himself has been benefited, perhaps had he not taken the first advice he would have been now suffering from some malady worse than the mere loss of his tonsils, perhaps he would not have been here at all."

The red corders nodded solemnly at this and gave some faint indications of applause. In the back seats the young man muttered "Rot," but the doctor was proceeding with his lecture and the young man and Truth were definitely squashed.

Jenkins sat in his seat wondering. Had the young man made any impression on the red corders or not? He thought not. They had come there determined to hear the doctor, determined to hear no one else. They were determined to believe in him and to refuse to believe anyone else. That was their attitude. The doctor went on.

"To compel people to be healthy and happy surely that is what the laws should aim at and while now having grown up in our present lax system of pleasing himself, the individual may feel it hard to have his liberty curtailed I look forward to the future in which the child having been brought up on scientific principles from the first will not miss what he has never had—his liberty. Yes, that is the ideal, ladies and gentlemen, the child, we shall begin with the child. We shall take him from the cradle, nay more we shall deal with the mother beforehand, so that his pre-natal welfare will be studied. In the future we shall no longer see the poor neglected child clinging to the hand of its slatternly mother and sucking at the noxious sweets she has in her ignorance bought for it. No! We shall see a little being, gently led by a sweet faced hospital nurse, his eyes carefully protected by glasses, his pearly teeth already stopped with gold and supported by plates. No dirty clothes to harbor disease about him, he is dressed in the neat and simple uniform provided by the State. And within his little frame has been as carefully tended, his tonsils removed he need not dread tonsillitis, his appendix taken away what cause has he to fear appendicitis, X-rayed every week, no disease can approach him unperceived. Vaccinated every year against smallpox, inoculated frequently for typhoid and all the murderous maladies that surround us, here is my ideal little citizen of the future. He faces life armed by Science against all ills. Is it not an inspiring picture?"

The doctor paused and beamed in a fatherly way as if the little monstrosity he had conjured up by his words were on the platform, before him.

The red corders gave some applause, there was dead silence at the back for a second, then a voice asked:

"What about his little legs and arms, Mister, has he got 'em still, or have they been sawn off and artificial ones hooked on?"

Loud laughter from all the back benches greeted this interruption. When it had subsided the doctor replied gravely:

"Certainly nothing would be done to remove his limbs unnecessarily, if on the other hand any accident happened to him there are artificial limbs in readiness so carefully thought out, so exquisitely fashioned that they function nearly as well as the natural ones."

"Rats!" came an angry voice from the wooden benches and a young man sprang to his feet. He looked like an ex-soldier, his face was pale and thin with a hectic flush burning on his cheek-bones. One sleeve hung empty by his side.

"Look at me!" he shouted, "I had my arm taken off in the war by some of you devils. Wasn't a bit necessary, ordinary nursing would have saved it. But what's that to you? You don't care for flesh and blood, you only care for your devilish devices. I had a flesh wound and off you took my arm and gave me a false one, a thing all straps and buckles and springs that tortured me like hell. I was kept on view and taught to pick up a pin when the Queen came to see me. What good's that to me? The whole thing fell to pieces after a week or two. You leave us alone and our children too. We don't want your spectacles and your false teeth and your X-rays. Leave our young 'uns alone as God made 'em. That's what I say." He sat down and all those at the back applauded loudly.

The doctor on the platform gave his shoulders an infinitesimal shrug and waited in silence until the storm had subsided. Then he continued in a pained voice, as one grieved by the deep ingratitude of the world.

"Again I can only say we must not judge from unfortunate exceptions. Artificial limbs are and have been and will always be a great boon to humanity."

"We prefer to keep our own, thank you!" retorted the young man, which remark the doctor passed over with a patient air and continued his lecture.

There was nothing new in it. The same old rubbish that is always set afloat by the doctors and scientific men and then repeated pompously from mouth to mouth without examination by the asses in society was duly brought forward here.

As the doctor himself with his usual cynicism would have remarked, "Why take the trouble to invent a new lie when you can still gull the public with the old one?"

He cited the great benefits that Science had conferred on humanity in the War, how inoculation had saved the troops from typhoid without explaining why a hundred thousand had died after Gallipoli.

He dilated on the wonderful advantages of the *X*-ray without mentioning the countless victims who had been slowly roasted to death under it.

He expatiated on anti-toxin cures of diphtheria without explaining why the death rate from diphtheria had gone up and not down since its use and without mentioning that Bella Donna is a specific for that disease and there is no need whatever for anti-toxin which involves the most hideous suffering to horses.

Lies and lies and more lies flowed from his lips until it seemed to Jenkins he got choked with them. A hurried sip of water and he brought his speech to a close with the usual appeal for more funds for Research, that noble work in which thousands of selfless men and women (like himself, he implied) were spending their lives. After that came some whisper and a little fluttering pause. Then the Chairman announced amidst applause from the red corders that a cheque for 50,000 pounds had been received from a member of the audience who wished to remain anonymous, for the splendid work—the direct result of the doctor's moving address.

With hissing and booing the company at the back got on to their feet and made for the doors.

Jenkins and his neighbour went out together. A line of well appointed, lighted motors stood outside. The two men paused as if with one accord and waited watching the well dressed crowd come out, get into their cars and roll smoothly away.

"There they go," keen-eyes said bitterly, "home to sleep in their downy beds or to eat and drink with never a thought of the agony of the poor suffering animals. Fools! Led by the nose by that criminal lunatic that's been telling them all that rubbish this evening. And they've *got* the brains to see through it all, that's what makes me so mad with them. It's not as if they were stupid or uneducated and *couldn't* think for themselves. They *won't* think." He stopped and drew a pipe from his pocket and began filling it and ramming in the tobacco. "I used to think well of the upper classes at one time. I know they are unselfish and they work hard lots of them and do a lot of good to others but the way they've swallowed all this cant about Scientific Research, the way they shut their eyes and ears to the truth has disgusted me with them. We've got regular devil-worship in England now. What these so-called scientific chaps do in their laboratories is appalling. It's just sheer lust of killing and torturing, lust run wild and those fools patronise it and *because* they patronise it, every man-jack in the Kingdom, got to pay for it. We've got to struggle along and pay taxes that fellows like this Smith-Brown may enjoy themselves wallowing in a horrible vice. I tell you I've read about devil-worship in Africa and whole communities being under the thumb of a few priests and we've jolly well got exactly the same thing going on in England to-day. The health of the country is being ruined, the blood and the brains of the people all messed up by the filthy inoculations and vaccinations and we are breeding more and more men with this lust in their brains for tearing living things to pieces and those people are responsible for all this." He jerked his thumb in the direction of the departing motors gliding away soundlessly bearing their freights of humanity, good hearted, kindly persons for the most part, but utterly blinded by a foolish and fanatical belief: just as completely as the simple savage peoples of darkest Africa are blinded by their medicine men when they order them to gash their breasts and throw their mutilated babies into the flames.

"What can we do?" pursued keen-eyes as the two men turned away into the darkness of the wet streets. "We're poor, we can't do anything. We can't get at the public to tell it what's going on. If we're ill we're lugged off to these beastly hospitals and cut up alive, we're forced to send our children to school and the doctors there cut'em about as they like, what can we do? But those people, they *could* alter things, one of those lords owns a newspaper, if he studied the thing up, he could set it all out in his paper and squash the whole thing. He could show up these scientific men and what they do. He could show that this whole craze for torturing animals was just a form of lunacy. The nation wouldn't support it for two minutes if it were once told what it was. But he does nothing, he uses his paper just to help the thing on. Then those other lords, they could speak in their House and say outright what it was—just devil-worship—but they allow themselves to be humbugged like all the rest of the fools."

After a pause keen-eyes started again in his quick fiery way.

"What I keep on hoping is that the medical profession itself will see what a mistake they are making. Already a number of doctors have declared themselves against experiments on animals. That's the root of the whole trouble. Experiments on living animals. The doctors are wrongly trained from the beginning. The young men, the medical students in their classes, at their lectures, see a living animal being operated upon, being cut up, before them. Sometimes it is under an anaesthetic, sometimes partially so, sometimes not at all. They are taught that this is right, they are trained to cut the animal up alive themselves. They are trained to see the animal writhing and struggling in its helpless agonies and shown how to inflict them. These men are young men, they are just at that age when the brain is most susceptible to impressions, when the character is forming, when there are terrible impulses towards evil and equally great yearnings toward good. It is quite easy to see what an effect these classes must have upon them, these spectacles of the living pulsating form of an animal being torn in pieces, by an older man, who is evidently absolutely indifferent to the horrible suffering he is causing. And this effect is evil. At first many of these young men do feel horror at the sight, they feel the normal sympathy everyone should feel at the sight of suffering. Then they are jeered at by their older companions. They are told that callous man who is sinking his knife between muscle and bone cutting the nerves of the poor moaning victim is doing *right* and a great man. Thus they are initiated into the devil worship. Sometimes the young students overcome by the revolt of all their natural instincts against it, faint at the revolting sight. They are carried out of the class room and revived. By the order of the professor they are brought back and *made* to witness the lingering torments of the animal on the operating-table They are being hardened. Day by day they are trained thus and gradually their normal feelings begin to change. From sickness and revolt at the horrors they see done, they come to a liking for them, a wish to participate in them, they become abnormal. Their brains having been shocked at the most sensitive age, they become deflected from their true balance. Those feelings of justice, mercy, sympathy and pity which distinguish the worthy human being disappear and the normal young man who commenced his medical course is at the end of it an abnormal ill balanced creature with that impulse towards cruelty we notice in the monkey highly developed and the qualities of man carefully trained out of his crooked brain. And it is from this material we make our doctors! The men we call in to treat our beloved sick, to minister to our dear ones when dying! Heavens, what a farce! Doctors above all men should be highly trained in sympathy and justice. Nothing should be allowed to cloud or shock the brain of the young medical student. A clear judgment, great power of observation, great sympathy with all suffering, reverence for life. These are the qualities we want in our doctors and should therefore be cultivated in our medical students. All that is necessary for the healing of the human body can be learned from the careful observation of that body in health and in sickness and in death. Anatomy can be far better taught by cutting up the dead human body than the living animal."

He stopped and there was silence between them as they plodded on. Jenkins felt too crushed and wretched to be able to collect his thoughts and he knew it was not safe for him, with his ultimate object in view, to reveal himself or his sentiments to anyone. He felt vaguely comforted by the companionship of this other man who evidently, like himself, knew the truth, but he dared not confide in him. He could only listen in silence. The other did not seem to mind. He appeared to know instinctively that Jenkins was of one mind with himself and he asked no questions. At the corner of Oxford Street he stopped and held out his hand.

"I wait here," he said, "my bus'll be along presently. Goodnight, it's a bad business but remember this, *it can't last*. The day will come when this gigantic fraud on the public, this Scientific Research, will be exposed. We mayn't be here to see it, worse luck, for it will take a long time but it must come. All frauds come to the same end."

Jenkins grasped his hand and wrung it, the kind keen eyes met his for a moment. Then they had parted and Jenkins was drifting down a side street alone with his hands driven down deep into the pockets of his overcoat and clenched there.

What *could* he do, what *could* he do to unveil this stupendous lie? To raise this flimsy curtain of a *name* and show the filthy loathsome lust that cowered behind it. He walked and walked desperately up one street and down another. He did not know or care where he went. He would walk through the night and only turn up at this loathsome work in the morning. The utter horror of the whole thing enveloped him like a cloud and his terrible impotence in the matter seemed like something stifling suffocating him. He believed he could kill the doctor and so save a certain amount of horrible suffering but that was so little against the whole mass of evil and error that a small band of men had managed to let loose upon the world. For the whole world was affected. This folly of blind belief in the words of men who dubbed themselves wise and learned, beneficent and infallible, had spread its sickly snare not over one country nor quarter but over the whole world. Hospitals, laboratories are found everywhere and though there were wise and thinking people also everywhere they did not seem numerous enough nor strong enough to stop the march of Evil. Would the day of deliverance ever come? He wondered dismally as keen-eyes had predicted. For the present this devil-worship was all on the up-grade. More taxes were being levied, more money thrown into the hands of the medicine men, more hospitals being built, more research laboratories being endowed. Jenkins wandered on through the damp, black streets depressed to the very uttermost. That lecture had pushed him down to the very depths of despair, just as Doctor Smith-Brown had cynically foreseen it would do. He saw that Jenkins had still some faith in the common sense of ordinary people. The doctor determined he should attend the lecture and see for himself how easily and completely they were taken in and deluded. Towards morning, stiff and aching in every limb he got back to the laboratory. It was dark and cold: fires and lights were out and a low moaning of unutterable anguish filled the darkness. Jenkins went heavily up the stairs to his bed, wretched beyond description, oppressed by the wickedness of one half of the world and the stupidity of the other half.

CHAPTER 5

Three weeks had elapsed, three weeks of dreadful mental suffering for Jenkins and it had left its mark upon him. He was a changed man from the one who came strong and straight, clear-eyed and tranquil-minded from the country. He had grown pale and gaunt, he stooped a little, his clothes hung on him loosely. Those sleepless nights when the screaming of the animals in mortal agony rang through the whole house penetrating even to his top room and through his blocked up ears, were draining his strength little by little, but now his resolve once fixed and the determination to kill the doctor, clear cut in his mind, he was less unhappy than in those first days of astounded wondering, crumbling beliefs and uncertainty as to where his duty lay.

Now that the Right lay plain before him, he had only one anxiety—that his strength would hold out until his duty was done. He walled himself round with a solid reserve and kept his grim purpose before him night and day. He realised that he could do very little. He knew that when a whole nation has gone mad and determined to set up a horrible vice in its midst and worship it, one individual has little power to avert the madness. He had learned by now that there were these hideous laboratories all over London that the tax-payers of England were burdened to support them, that there were numbers of men afflicted with the same monomania as the doctor and whose work equalled in barbarity his though it could not exceed it. He knew all this, but in those horrible nights hearing the beseeching cries of the tortured animals below, he reasoned thus. Each of these scientific researchers is responsible for killing in agony a certain number of animals. He had heard for instance the doctor quote a French surgeon who boasted he had done to death eight thousand dogs in his laboratory. He argued, therefore, if he could remove even one of these dehumaned human beings from the world, he would certainly save a few thousand helpless animals from torture and Jenkins felt that was quite worth while. Of what use was this silly semi-demented old man who sat in his laboratory dabbling in the blood of dogs or writing to the newspapers about ridiculous cures he had discovered, that when tried were found to be no cures at all, or mixing his filthy glycerine in order to cultivate his still more filthy germs in it? Jenkins, not being one of the befooled public, saw very clearly that men like this one were not suppressing disease but spreading it: that these laboratories were plague spots where not new remedies, but new diseases were invented and elaborated.

The doctor was quite mad, Jenkins was convinced of that and as there seemed no way of conveying him to an asylum where he belonged it would be well to remove him altogether from this world where he was doing so much evil not only to the animals but to Mankind.

Therefore waiting and watching for his opportunity Jenkins went quietly day by day about his work, suffering inwardly horribly for the poor mutilated animals he had to tend, but letting no sign of agitation or distress appear in his sedate and stoic manner. The doctor from time to time eyed him curiously noting with grim satisfaction the physical changes that had taken place in his hard-working attendant. He was quite aware that Jenkins was more or less against his work and felt pain in seeing the tortures of the animals, and therefore his evil mind delighted in forcing him to witness the most brutal experiments. Such as tearing out a dog's eyes to transplant them to another or cutting out an ear by the roots and sewing it into the victim's neck. He knew also that Jenkins saw through the whole farce and that he could not deceive his attendant as he did the easy going public, so he no longer pretended that these experiments had any use in them. At the end of a loathsome exhibition of suffering and torture which had especially gratified his perverted sexuality, he would turn his gloating face with its protruding eyes and saliva covered lips to Jenkins and dig him playfully in the ribs.

"Good work that, eh, Jenkins? Not exactly useful, but interesting, eh? Let's say *interesting*," and Jenkins, a wooden figure with a wooden face would stand there with the fires of just indignation burning him to death within and exerting all his mental and moral force to keep himself from striking down the fiend in front of him.

So the days passed for the two men, shut away from the world in their little building on the piece of waste ground by the common—playfully for the doctor who "loved his work" as he was never tired of informing the newspapers. He did indeed love his work and wallowed in its atrocity as a drunkard in his cups. It was the only true thing he ever said but that was true, he loved his work— painfully for Jenkins who thought each night he could bear his martyrdom no longer. But at last the end came.

Jenkins had had a peculiarly sickening afternoon: dog after dog had been taken: thrown in the vivisecting trough, wrenched and racked and torn, its nerves stimulated, red hot irons passed through its most sensitive parts and finally been thrown in shrieking agony into a corner. The doctor was enjoying himself, that he loved his work was very evident from his excited face, from which he occasionally wiped the sweat and then resumed his task with fresh ardour. Six o'clock struck and the doctor stopped.

"Done a good day's work, I think," he remarked. "Take 'em away, Jenkins, kill 'em if you like. I've done with them. I'll have a fresh lot to-morrow," and he waved his hand to the mangled heap on the stone floor in the corner from which long gasping shivering cries were rising. "I'm going out. Go upstairs and get your tea. I shan't want you again till to-morrow." With that he turned to his dressing room from which Jenkins knew he would soon emerge, calm, collected, bland, immaculate, the suave man of Science that he appeared in public.

Before getting his tea, Jenkins turned to see what could be done for the poor bleeding remnants of living beings in the heap. Alas, nothing but to quiet them in death. He bent over them despatching them as gently and as quickly as he could and in half an hour the last poor battered thing had expired. Just then the doctor came out smooth and sleek and genially smiling. Well dressed as always and holding a little paper in his hand.

"I'm thinking of making a few remarks to-night on the benefit of Vivisection. Some old faddists are getting up on their hind legs and saying it shouldn't be allowed, so it's best to give the public our usual little dose of talk."

Jenkins, sick to death, just nodded and went on with his task of carrying out the dead bodies. Then suddenly as the lightning flashes the moment was upon him and the whole man's spirit sprang to attention and every fibre within him quivered for action. On his way out the doctor paused by the door of the lethal chamber and Jenkins on his way back for another body, found him standing in the hallway sniffing delicately about him.

"There's a queer smell here," he remarked. "I don't like it. Where does it come from?"

As he spoke he turned the handle, pushed open the door, of the lethal room, and—entered. Jenkins, the blood stinging in all his veins and a great light in his brain, moved forward. He was not conscious of movement, only of intention. Equally without consciousness of the action, his arm shot out, his lean fingers gripped the handle. The brain had had standing orders given it long ago and now the moment had come, like lightning it obeyed.

The heavy door swung to and clicked. It was shut and no earthly power could open it from within. There was no sound. Silence fell on the laboratory. The instant the door had closed Jenkins became a different man. The great deed for which he had lived night and day was done, swiftly and successfully accomplished. He held his head high. His heart swelled within him with a joyous sense of duty done just as when he had walked out of the enlisting office in August, 1914, a soldier proud to die for his country. So now if he had to die on the scaffold for this night's work he would die proudly for he knew that the work was good. One liar, one duper of the public, one traitor to his country, *one* monster of cruelty, if but one, had been put out of existence. A great flood of joy seemed to engulf him and he stalked forward to the pipes and tubes to turn on the taps that let in to the chamber the deadly gasses.

It was but the work of a few minutes, for the useful chamber was always kept in readiness by the doctor. It might be some unexpected visitor might call at the moment when an animal was screaming under the doctor's fingers and then the quickest way to obtain silence was to throw it into the lethal room out of the way before the visitor was admitted. Of course if it were a man of Science such a precaution was unnecessary because he would understand that the piercing cries only meant his fellow worker was "loving his work" and pursuing it as usual but it might be an ordinary person who called and then ordinary people take a different view of these things and have to be humbugged accordingly.

Jenkins stalked to the tubes and turned the taps full on. There were no merciful air holes in this chamber arranged so that the air might mix with the burning gasses and the victim may be overcome by the mixed fumes instead of being choked and burnt to death. No, the doctor wouldn't have air holes and when Jenkins had pointed out to him how twisted and contorted the bodies were that he had to remove pointing to the fact that a very painful death had been experienced, the doctor had gazed at him over his cigarette smoke with a mild reflective gaze for a few seconds and then had turned away without a word. The air holes had never been made and a grim smile hovered for a moment over the attendant's impassive face as he turned on the gas and then walked away down the passage to the stairway where he sat down on the lowest stair ... waiting, while the minutes passed. Then suddenly the three dogs in the reserve room broke into loud and joyous barking. Jenkins listened astonished. He had never heard them do that before. No animal within those walls ever lifted its voice except to wail in agony. But now? Did they know their hideous persecutor was dead? Could they see the spirit passing? Animals have many higher gifts than man: many instincts, many powers that are denied to him; or that he has destroyed by his vices, which they are without. And their nearness to the spiritual world had often struck Jenkins before. This was extraordinary. He could hear them bounding and scuffling about in the room giving short sharp barks of joy. Jenkins first thought was to go in but with his hand on the door knob he paused. He had only just lately had their dead companions in his arms. He would go and take off his blood stained garments before meeting them, get rid of the scent of death which they would recognize so well but he had something to do first. He must put out of their long long suffering those poor unfortunates that awaited in the ghastly gallery the morrow's torture. He switched on the lights and then entered the gallery, where the scientist had pursued the work he loved. Jenkins could not bear to meet the sad, glazing eyes that stared dully at him through the bars of those cruel cages. What would he not have given to have been able to restore the joyous healthy forms they had possessed before the Scientist had cut and beaten and mangled and starved them out of all resemblance to living creatures. But he was helpless, man can destroy but he cannot create an animal.

At last it was over. All life was extinguished and the many mangled forms lay stretched on the cold zinc floors of their cages where they had dragged out their existence of months and years of suffering. Jenkins gave one glance round: his hands and feet cold but his heart burning like a red hot coal within him.

"This place justifies me," he thought, "if anything is needed, this place alone is my excuse."

Then he switched out the lights and death and darkness reigned supreme in the place of agony.

Coming out into the hall, he heard the joyous voices of the living dogs and his face cleared a little of its gloom. He walked to the lethal chamber and turned off the tap. Then he hurried up to his own little flat and there soon had stove and lamp well alight. He washed and changed his clothes rapidly. It was wonderful how light and strong he felt. Some great pressure in the atmosphere was removed now that he knew that evil thing was safely locked in the chamber below. Where had the evil spirit gone? Jenkins did not know nor care. If it were about in the house any where still Jenkins was not afraid of it.

His conscience was so absolutely clear, his heart, his brain, all his instincts told him he was right, that he had done well. He felt certain that any decent man watching that fiend working day by day would have acted as he had done, if he had stayed his hand so long. Most men in his place would have jumped on the doctor and strangled him when he first realised what the so-called scientist really was. No good man who knew the truth would condemn him so his heart was light and he had no fear of the doctor's ghost. He would have met it cheerfully and give it some straight talk had it ventured up the stairs.

But no ghost or spirit came and Jenkins hurried along over his dressing and then made his long belated tea. Then with an armful of dog biscuits and a great jug of milk he descended to the expectant four foots below.

The lights were burning and the place looked cosy and cheery enough. The lethal room was there solid and silent guarding well its secrets and the welcoming bark of the dogs hearing his footsteps resounded through the hall. Jenkins opened the door and immediately out bounded the dogs leaping up to and caressing him. He saw at once the difference in them. Up to now a horror and terror had seemed to brood over them: it was in the air of the whole place, never had they ventured before uninvited into the hall. What they smelt, what they heard in that accursed place had told them frightful things, though Jenkins had guarded them all he could from that knowledge.

Now they capered about the hall unrestrained and leapt up at Jenkins' side as if acclaiming him and welcoming him as their master. Jenkins, too sad at heart for his frolicsome companion to wholly cheer, went into their room soberly and filled all their saucers to the brim and broke their biscuits with careful fingers. After all it was so little that he had done! Just one of these men stopped from their horrible work, only one out of so many. Yet little actions sometimes had widespreading results. He wondered sadly whether by the voluntary sacrifice of his life he could do anything, by giving himself up and telling plainly and boldly his whole story in the dock to judge and jury, would he accomplish anything? Would Judge and Jury listen and believe? No, he thought not, they would be just like the lady to whom he had restored the cat. A personal motive would be ascribed to him for his act and Judge and Jury would only listen to the crowd of scientists who would pack the court. They would tell the judge and jury that animals did not feel, that when cut up alive it was done with the greatest kindness that the vivisectors who were appointed to inspect these places would certainly not sympathise with vivisectors working these, that Sir Charles Smith-Brown, Dsc. M.D., L.R.C.P., etc., etc., was the kindest man that ever breathed, that he lived only to benefit humanity and all these lies would be believed and all this absurd nonsense swallowed and Jenkins' plain truth set aside and Jenkins hanged. That would be all. As for the newspapers they would not report a word of what Jenkins said but only what the scientists said by whom they were paid. No to keep his life if possible and gradually try to disseminate the truth was the only way that offered any hope. There must be some thinking men and women in England. They could not all be maundering fools like those that sat in Parliament and babbled about "effective inspection of laboratories" by vivisectors and voted huge sums of money for cancer research, *i.e.*, for infecting thousands of animals with cancer, for cultivating cancer, and thus spreading the disease through the length and breadth of the land.

No, he decided, slightly comforted, they couldn't all be fools! There must be some common sense left in England somewhere. He must try to find it and appeal to it.

The dogs' supper over, he let them out for a run and then proceeded on his rounds as usual to see all was closed for the night. There were some letters for the doctor in the letter box and these he took out and arranged carefully on the table under a green shaded lamp in the doctor's own special little study, the door of which was just opposite the door of the lethal chamber on the other side of the hall.

He turned out all the lights and locked all the outer doors except the hall door which "the doctor would open with his latch key when he returned."

Jenkins felt the value of knowing his story beforehand and he was from now on going to entirely forget that the doctor's body lay in the lethal chamber. When it was eventually dragged out, it must be a surprise to him. He had been told by the doctor that the latter was going out and that he might go upstairs to his tea. That was at 6 o'clock. He had availed himself of the permission and gone upstairs leaving the doctor in the hall. He had not seen him since and when he came down he concluded that the doctor had gone out and not returned. That was going to be his story and he was going to act in every particular as if were a true one. So he ranged the letters carefully under the lamp tidied the doctor's papers and left everything in order for his return.

At ten he went to the main door and whistled in the dogs, saw them to their beds with many caresses, then rather wearily sought his own.

But there was quiet and peace waiting for him to-night. No shrieks, no groans, the dead and the living alike side by side slept soundly that night in the laboratory.

CHAPTER 6

Six days had elapsed and the laboratory still stood silent without a master. Jenkins moved about in it silently as a ghost, doing everything exactly as he would have done had he expected the doctor's return any minute. He had sent the three dogs down into the country by train to the man who kept an eye on his little cottage while he was away and who would look after them. Inwardly he was longing for it all to be over, longing to leave this accursed spot where he had gone through such horrible suffering. His work was all done there now. Every cage in the long corridor had been thoroughly cleaned out: the bars polished: the floor washed and the tiles of the corridor itself swabbed over and rubbed to a glistening cleanliness. The doctor's rooms were kept swept and dusted and each day's letters as they came in were ranged in neat order on his writing table, with a little space between each day's group. The fires were lighted in the morning, the lamps lighted in the evening.

Jenkins waited up till ten o'clock each night. Then solemnly switched off the lights and retired. He was pale and gaunt but not unhappy now, as compared with his former days here. He had done what he could. It was not much but it was something, and perhaps work lay ahead for him in the future. Perhaps he could be instrumental in exposing this awful vice, this cruel murderous lust that called itself Scientific Research. He missed the three dogs enormously but here again he hugged himself with pleasure in thinking they were safe and out of the way.

It was just five on the Saturday evening and Jenkins was downstairs taking his tea in the dogs' room where he kept now his little outfit for tea making, that he might be at hand to open the door. A ring came and he rose at once to answer.

"Sir C. Smith-Brown at home?" queried the thin-lipped young man who stood outside.

"No, sir."

"Oh. When do you expect him back?"

"Any time, sir. He has not been in this week: not since Monday evening."

"Really? I wonder where he is then. I don't seem able to catch him anywhere. Did he say he was going into the country or anything?"

Jenkins shook his head.

"No, sir. He just left on Monday about six and said he wouldn't want me again that day. I expected him next morning but he didn't come and I haven't seem him since."

"Funny! You've been here all the time I suppose?"

"Oh, yes, sir, I never go out unless the doctor gives me special leave to."

"Well, I'll look up Dr. Jones and see if he's there. Thanks, good night."

The young man departed. Jenkins closed the door and went back to the dogs' room where he reboiled his kettle and made himself another cup of tea.

"That's the beginning," he thought to himself. "Now there'll be a disagreeable time I expect, and after that I'll be free I hope," and he smiled to himself as he thought of the rescued dogs waiting for him in the country.

Jenkins was right. The search for the doctor had begun. At nine thirty, a longer more peremptory ring sounded through the house accompanied by a knock. He went at once to the door. The thin-lipped young man was there but this time in company with a shortish rotund man who made up for his insignificant stature with great pomposity of manner. As soon as the door was opened he stepped over the threshold with a hint of defiance in his bearing as if he expected an effort on the part of Jenkins to keep him out and had determined it should be unsuccessful. Jenkins inwardly amused immediately stepped back having opened the door to its fullest extent.

"This seems a serious affair about your master," began his visitor. "He is not at his house, he is not at his hospital, and you say he is not here." There was the faintest accent laid on the "you say." Jenkins looked gravely interested.

"When did you see him last?"

"Monday evening, sir, about six."

"He's not been back since, not even looked in, eh?"

"No, sir, I don't think he could have. All his letters are here." He stepped to the study door and threw it open, switching on the light. The neat cosy little room stood revealed very orderly. On the table under the green shaded lamp lay the doctor's letters ranged in their little groups according to the day of their arrival.

The doctor's chair was drawn toward the hearth, neatly swept up where a small fire burnt primly.

The two visitors peered into the room, the rotund Dr. Jones went up to the table and fingered one or two of the letters as if he hoped to gain information from them.

"Such an exact man, such a precise man, I can't understand his going off like this for six days and telling nobody."

He stared hard at Jenkins who returned his gaze with a slightly distressed expression but made no reply.

"Well, I think I and my friend would like just to look through the place," Jones continued, his manner something between embarrassment and aggression.

"We should feel more satisfied you know and something might strike us as a clue to his disappearance."

Jenkins assented at once.

"Do, sir, will you go round alone or shall I come with you?"

"Oh, you come along by all means," Jones answered and the three of them came out of the study into the hall again. Jenkins opened the next door that of the cold long gallery where the agonized animals had suffered such hideous miseries. Here there were no fires: the air was deadly chill and still foul, or so it seemed to Jenkins, the electric light fell wanly on the white walls, the lofty arched roof and the cold glistening tiles of the floor.

Jones advanced. Then stopped short with an exclamation as his eye caught the long row of empty silent cages.

"What's this? Got rid of his animals? Why that looks as if he knew he were not coming back! What do you thing of that Edward?" he addressed his companion.

"Looks like it," he replied laconically.

"When did the doctor dispose of his animals?" asked Jones wheeling round upon Jenkins.

"He'd been using them up for some time, sir," answered Jenkins, "and last week he said he'd finish with all he'd got and have a fresh stock in and I was to clean out all the cages and have them ready for a new lot."

"Oh, he said that, did he?" returned Jones. "Hm—hm—hm. Well, let's go on down to the end. See if he's left a note or anything on the table."

The three men filed down the cold long room to the end where behind the screen which helped to shut this part off from the corridor stood the doctor's armchair close to the hearth. The heavy writing table was covered with papers all neatly piled and arranged. Everything was neat and in order all most carefully dusted. The large inkstand carefully polished and a tray of freshly nibbed pens awaited the doctor's return. Evidently his servant had expected him back.

Dr. Jones looked disconsolately over the table. There was no note or letter there. The last thing apparently that the doctor had written was a chemical equation, drawn out on a half sheet of notepaper. This lay on the blotting pad, carefully preserved by the invaluable Jenkins.

Dr. Jones looked at it and then laughed. To those who know how to read the ciphers it represented a burning solution, designed to separate living flesh from living bone.

"Well nothing here, Edward, we'll go upstairs," and following Jenkins, upstairs they went. They tramped through the doctor's comfortable little suite above, looking in cupboards and under the bed and finding nothing but order and extreme cleanliness everywhere.

After that Jenkins' rooms were entered and searched but the simple furniture and narrow bed were soon looked over and under. The dog's room, the bathroom, the landings the little coal cellar: they searched all most thoroughly expecting as it seemed to Jenkins to find the doctor's body concealed somewhere and possibly swinging behind some door. Dr. Jones seemed to have jumped to the conclusion that it was a case of suicide.

"I can't understand his stopping all his experiments and giving up all the animals like that," Jenkins heard him remark to his friend. "Looks like suicide, 'pon my word it does."

Their search yielded nothing however and at last with a curt goodnight to Jenkins they left, passing by the lethal chamber on their way out.

"Fools," thought Jenkins as he closed the door after them.

After that there was no more tranquility at the laboratory. The bell was frequently being rung, people came to enquire, Jenkins was interviewed by various persons, asked the same questions over and over again and told the same lies in answer with commendable consistency.

The papers now had got hold of the story and devoted large spaces to the mysterious disappearance of the famous scientist. Reporters came to see Jenkins and to hear repeated the few simple sentences he could tell them. But to these reporters he added to his story accounts of the doctor's doings and took the reporters in to see the vivisecting troughs and all the ghastly instruments of torture that are the stock in trade of the Scientific Researcher. But though they looked open eyed and open mouthed on these gruesome objects and wandered up and down the long gallery reading the incriminating labels on the empty cages never a word of any of these things appeared in their reports in the papers as Jenkins vainly hoped.

In talking to them, he naturally had to preserve the stolid indifference of manner that had been his mask so long and appear to think all this scientific atrocity in order and he could feel that even these light headed and unthinking young men shrank away from him in loathing. At such times Jenkins would feel a madness of longing to shake them by the hand and urge them to carry his message to the world but all this he crushed down. To show the least disapprobation of the doctor's doings, to be anything but the servile laboratory attendant would attract suspicion to himself, perhaps fasten the noose round his neck. So he bore their evident contempt and disgust with himself as he had borne all the rest of his sufferings in that place without a sign and in their attitude to him he had a certain rejoicing. It gave a glimmer of hope for the future.

"Catch me giving a penny of *my* money to Cancer Research after this," he heard one of the men say to his companion as they went out and his heart warmed with hope.

Alas! the next morning in the very paper which had sent these two to report there was a glowing article upon the doctor's work, his superb labours for humanity and all the rest of the unutterable twaddle with which Jenkins was by now so familiar. Days passed and still nothing was heard of the eminent scientist, the Press made all they could out of his disappearance, it was the favorite topic of the clubs and dinner parties. He had simply vanished and public interest and excitement skilfully fanned by the papers waxed and grew.

On the second Saturday after his disappearance just when Editors were thinking out a new headline, the favorite Possible Clue found to the Smith-Brown Mystery, having been rather overworked the end came abruptly.

At nine in the morning Jenkins opened the door to a small group of men led by a man in an inconspicuous uniform.

"I am a police inspector and have a warrant to search these premises."

"Yes, sir," returned Jenkins simply. There was nothing very new in that. "This is the doctor's study sir," he said, throwing open the door as he had done before for Dr. Jones.

The Inspector just glanced that way. Then he stepped up to the door on the other side of the hall.

"What's this?"

Jenkins turned back to him.

"That's the lethal chamber, sir."

The Inspector put his hand on the handle, turned it and pushed the door. It resisted and as he pushed it more there was the soft heavy sound of some inert thing being moved within.

"Stand back, gentlemen, please," he said as the little group pressed forward, and turned his electric torch into the black aperture made by the partially opened door. The white light gushed in and its broad streak fell on the large head and upturned face of the doctor. Mouth wide open as he died gasping, eyes bulging in a last grisley stare. There was a gasp of horror from the onlookers as they drew back, a sickly odour stealing out from the little room and enveloping them.

The Inspector seemed the only man unmoved. He ordered one of his men to support the door that it should not close and two others to follow him. Then he went in and the three of them brought out the doctor's body between them into the hall and laid it down. It was horribly contorted as if the man had died writhing.

Jenkins turned away. He knew the look so well, just so all knotted with agony, had the poor little monkeys been when he drew them out from where they had huddled against the door or walls. The Inspector touched his arm.

"This must be very painful to you," he said kindly, touched by the woebe-gone look of Jenkins' gaunt wasted face.

"We do not need you for the moment. I shall have some questions to ask you presently but don't stand here now. Go into the next room and sit down."

"Thank you, sir," replied Jenkins brokenly and went.

Nothing could have been better nor convinced the Inspector more completely of his entire innocence of any participation in the doctor's death but it was not pose on Jenkin's part. In truth, physically he felt he could not stand much more of nervous strain and mentally he felt actually crushed with grief, though it was not as the Inspector supposed for his master, but for the countless little victims that master had so wantonly destroyed.

After a time the Inspector came to him and examined him. He questioned him and cross-questioned him but Jenkins made no mistakes. His short simple sentences, his direct replies, his simple manner, even his wooden face all to-gether produced the impression of a man, unlikely to do anything exceptional and original. He seemed to be the typical routine worker and wholly unconnected with the tragic event of his master's death.

At the inquest a verdict of Death from Misadventure, the doctor having been overcome by the old gas fumes remaining in the unventilated chamber, was re-turned and Jenkins after his evidence was allowed to leave for his home, unsus-pected and unopposed.

Down in his tiny cottage, one evening, before a blazing fire, where his three dogs lay extended in dozing comfort, sitting by the table with his pot of tea be-side him, he was somewhat laboriously reading a dull newspaper until his eyes caught these astounding head lines:

New Crusade for the Churches. 1,000,000 pounds appeal. Science and Reli-gion to co-operate.

Looking through the article he gathered that clergymen in all the churches were to preach to their congregations on the beauty and virtue of Scientific Re-search and raise a million pounds to be spent upon it. It was stated their scheme had the warm approval of the doctors. A little lower down he came on this para-graph:

"There is no more noble example of selfless service on behalf of humanity than the men and women engaged in Research work," and a little lower down still these same men and women were described as "dedicated spirits giving themselves as instruments into the hands of God, that His Will may be done upon Earth."

After reading this Jenkins sat back in his chair and remembered the doctor giving measles to his monkeys, filling cats with water till they burst and infecting healthy animals with cancer which never becomes human cancer and starving dogs to give them rickets.

"And the church now is going to help," he muttered. "Good Lord and Good Lord and Good Lord—"